Praise for *OCDaniel*

★ "King creates convincing characters and writes engaging dialogue, and whether or not readers identify fully with Daniel, they'll see parts of themselves in this vulnerable protagonist. . . . Written from Daniel's point of view, this perceptive first-person narrative is sometimes painful, sometimes amusing, and always rewarding." —*Booklist*, starred review

"Daniel's pain and confusion at what he comes to realize is OCD is memorably portrayed in this moving story of self-acceptance." —*Publishers Weekly*

"Daniel's narration is charming, funny, and occasionally heartbreaking, and a secondary cast of well-developed characters keeps the plot moving. . . . Part coming-of-age, part mystery, and part middle-grade social-problem novel, Daniel's story will resonate with a broad spectrum of readers." —*Kirkus Reviews*

"Daniel's a likable narrator who may well prompt readers to look around at their ever-so-slightly eccentric classmates with a bit more imagination and compassion." —*Bulletin*

Also by Wesley King

The Incredible Space Raiders from Space!

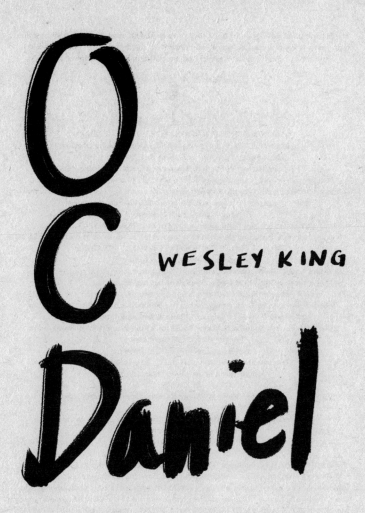

OCDaniel

WESLEY KING

A Paula Wiseman Book

Simon & Schuster Books for Young Readers

NEW YORK LONDON TORONTO SYDNEY NEW DELHI

SIMON & SCHUSTER BOOKS FOR YOUNG READERS
An imprint of Simon & Schuster Children's Publishing Division
1230 Avenue of the Americas, New York, New York 10020

This book is a work of fiction. Any references to historical events, real people, or real places are used fictitiously. Other names, characters, places, and events are products of the author's imagination, and any resemblance to actual events or places or persons, living or dead, is entirely coincidental.

SIMON & SCHUSTER BOOKS FOR YOUNG READERS
is a trademark of Simon & Schuster, Inc.
For information about special discounts for bulk purchases, please contact Simon & Schuster Special Sales at 1-866-506-1949 or business@simonandschuster.com.
The Simon & Schuster Speakers Bureau can bring authors to your live event. For more information or to book an event, contact the Simon & Schuster Speakers Bureau at 1-866-248-3049 or visit our website at www.simonspeakers.com.
Also available in a Simon & Schuster Books for Young Readers hardcover edition
Interior design by Hilary Zarycky
Cover art direction by Krista Vossen
The text for this book was set in ITC New Baskerville Std.
Manufactured in the United States of America
0617 OFF
First Simon & Schuster Books for Young Readers paperback edition April 2017
4 6 8 10 9 7 5 3
The Library of Congress has cataloged the hardcover edition as follows:
Names: King, Wesley.
Title: OCDaniel / Wesley King.
Other titles: OC Daniel
Description: New York : Simon & Schuster Books for Young Readers, [2016] | "A Paula Wiseman Book." | Summary: A thirteen-year-old Boy's life revolves around hiding his obsessive compulsive disorder until a girl at school, who is unkindly nicknamed Psycho Sara, notices him for the first time and he gets a mysterious note that changes everything.
Identifiers: LCCN 2015029259| ISBN 9781481455312 (hardback) | ISBN 9781481455336 (eBook)
Subjects: | CYAC: Obsessive-compulsive disorder—Fiction. | Mental Illness—Fiction. | Adventure and adventurers—Fiction. | BISAC: JUVENILE FICTION / Action & Adventure / General. | JUVENILE FICTION / Social Issues / Depression & Mental Illness. | JUVENILE FICTION / Science Fiction.
Classification: LCC PZ7.K58922 Oc 2016 | DDC [Fic]—dc23 LC record available at http://lccn.loc.gov/2015029259
ISBN 978-1-4814-5532-9 (pbk)

For OCD sufferers,
hope is rarely found alone

OCDaniel

CHAPTER 1

I first realized I was crazy on a Tuesday. I mean, I suspected it before, obviously, but I'd been hoping it was just a phase, like when I was three and I wanted to be a fire truck. But on that fateful October day she said hello after the last bell, and it was official—I was completely bonkers.

Tuesdays are usually my favorite day of the week. It's a weird day to like, but for me, a gangly, eccentric thirteen-year-old social oddity with only one real friend, it has some serious perks.

For one thing, we don't have football practice. Most kids probably like football practice, but when you're the backup kicker, you mostly just sit there and watch bigger, stronger kids run into each other and incur lifelong brain trauma. I know they're still studying that and all, but just talk to Dale Howard for a few minutes, and you can pretty much put a yellow warning label on the helmets.

Sometimes I get the team Gatorade—actually, I carefully arrange the cups into perfect geometric patterns to simplify drinking and reduce potential spillage—but that's the only fun part. Usually I just sit on the bench by myself and think about what would happen if aliens attacked the field and started laying radioactive eggs in the end zone. Or if flesh-eating monsters that only ate football players emerged from the ground and chased Coach Clemons. Or if we were attacked by an evil supervillain named Klarg who shot fire out of his eyeballs and was strangely vulnerable to orange Gatorade, which of course I had in huge supply. You get the idea.

The result is always the same: I save the world and never have to go to football practice again.

You might be asking why I go to football practice at all. The problem is that my dad; my older brother, Steve; and my best friend, Max, all love football and may stop talking to me altogether if I quit. I think I'm already pushing my luck with Max, so I just keep on playing. Or sitting on the bench, anyway.

I do some other stuff at practice too, but those are harder to explain. Like count the players and tie my shoes a lot and rearrange the cups after they're messed up. I think those are all fairly standard bored activities, at least for me. I do lots of things like that. Not really sure why. I spend most of my time hiding them from other people, so I can't exactly ask what's standard.

By the way, my name is Daniel Leigh. That's like "lee," not "lay." People get that wrong sometimes. I did say I was a thirteen-year-old social oddity, which is true. Actually I'm not sure what else to add. People say I'm smart, and I was in the Gifted Program when I was younger, until they got rid of it because it was a bit confusing to tell the other kids that some students were gifted and they weren't. Also I think they realized that if they continued the Gifted Program, us "gifted kids" would be separated our whole lives, but that happened anyway, so big deal.

I don't even know what being "gifted" means. I remember things easily and read novels every night, but that doesn't mean I'm smarter than Tom Dernt, who prefers to play football and is now superpopular. My teachers say I have a huge vocabulary and write way above my age level, but my brother told me to stop using fancy words or I'd never get a girlfriend. He has a girlfriend, so I have little choice but to heed his advice. I mean *take* his advice.

I also like to write. In fact, I am writing a book right now, though I don't tell anyone that—even my parents. I don't really want to share it, which will probably be an issue if I ever want to be published. It's called *The Last Kid on Earth*. It's an adventure story about a boy named Daniel.

Cryptic, I know. I have written the first page fifty-two times, and I am still not happy with it.

Oh, I also get distracted a lot and go on tangents. Which means I talk a lot about things you probably don't care about, so how is that smart? Let's get back to Tuesdays.

Geography is my last class of the day. It's one of my favorite subjects and rarely results in homework, since the long-suffering Mr. Keats usually just gives up on us and creates a work period so he can sit behind his desk and read the paper. There's no math that day either—another bonus, since I really stink at math. So no football, no homework, and, to make things better, Max usually comes over to play video games since his mom gets home late from work that night. Like I said, Tuesdays are the best. Well . . . usually. This Tuesday was not so great.

As usual, I was sitting next to Max, who was busy going on about our impending football game on Saturday morning against the Whitby Wildcats. He's on the team too, but he actually plays. Max is the tight end, which is way more important than the backup kicker—though, in fairness, so is every other position on the field. Of course, Max tends to forget that I don't even really like the sport and talks about it twenty times a day, but that's all right. We've been best friends since kindergarten, and he didn't ditch me when he got cool in the fifth grade and I didn't. In fact, being friends with him even keeps me on the distant fringe of the popular crowd, where I would never be otherwise. I'm like the guy the cool kids know but wouldn't actually call directly. That's better than being the guy who gets shoved into a locker, who I definitely would have been otherwise.

In any case, on that fateful day we were sitting in geography class and he was talking about football, and I was looking at Raya. Raya is a girl that we hang out with. Well, Max does. I hang out with Max, who hangs out with Raya. She's this cool girl who's really mature and way too pretty to look at the backup kicker of the Erie Hills Elephants. Yeah, not a great football name. We do this whole trunk thing before games. Never mind.

Back to Raya. She wears clothes that don't even make sense—cardigans and shawls and Technicolor stuff that aren't usually considered cool. I think. I wear T-shirts and hoodies that my mom gets at Walmart, so I'm not exactly a fashion expert, though I read plenty of articles online in case Raya ever asks me about it. For instance I know that men should really wear fitted dress shirts and pants with pleats if they want to look successful and attract women. I considered it for a while, but my brother told me that he would personally beat me up if I went to school with pleated khakis, so I just kept wearing hoodies. I also know that some Parisian fashion designers still use ivory, which I find upsetting because it means they are killing elephants for a necklace that could easily be made out of plastic. I like elephants.

They're clever, compassionate, and reportedly remember everything, though I can't confirm that. I'll try to stay focused.

Raya's hair is cut pretty short, and it always looks supertrendy and is usually died red or something. But I really don't care about any of that stuff. Okay . . . her eyes are really nice—they look like hot chocolate with marshmallows circling the mug, which is one of my favorite beverages. And she has a pretty smile that leans just a little to the right, revealing one of those pointy fang teeth. Those are just evolutionary remainders from our ancestors biting into sinewy raw meat and muscles, but for Raya the pointy fang teeth are perfect.

She is also smart and funny, and she has this little dimple that deepens on her right cheek when she laughs. How long had I been staring again?

"You're being a weirdo," Max said, nudging my arm.

"What?"

He sighed. "Case and point, Space Cadet."

Max calls me Space Cadet, by the way. I do this thing where my eyes glaze over and I stare at stuff and don't realize I'm doing it.

"You know, she has her flaws," Max said.

My infatuation with Raya Singh was well documented.

"No she doesn't," I said defensively.

"She does," Max insisted. "Most important, she doesn't like you."

"How do you know that?"

"A hunch."

I turned back to Raya and slumped, defeated. "You're probably right."

Max leaned in conspiratorially. "But you'll never know unless you ask."

I almost laughed. The class was kind of whispering to each other anyway, but a laugh might have been a bit too much and drawn unwanted attention. Mr. Keats was writing some stuff on the whiteboard, and we were supposed to be taking notes. I think a few people were, and I kind of wanted to, but Max always advised me that it was way cooler to not copy the notes. Worse for tests, though, I always noticed.

Max didn't always give me the best advice. He was like a cooler version of me. He was lean and muscular, with closely cropped black hair and piercing blue eyes. Girls liked him, though he seemed a bit leery of them, which he probably picked up from me. I was flat-out terrified of girls. Especially Raya.

"What should I ask her?" I said. "'Raya, do you like me?'"

He shrugged. "Sounds about right."

I looked at Max incredulously. "That was sarcasm."

"Oh. Well, I would just try it. What do you have to lose?"

"My dignity, pride, and self-respect." I paused. "Point taken."

I sighed and shifted my gaze to the whiteboard, where

Mr. Keats had finally stopped writing notes and was now looking out at the class in disapproval. If I had to describe him in fashion terms, it would be striped button-down shirts buttoned to the top and pleated khakis. Oh . . . my brother was right.

Written at the bottom of the board was:

Geography Test: THIS Friday, October 19th. STUDY, PLEASE.

Frowning, I picked up my pen and wrote the date down. At least I started to.

As I began writing "19th," my pen abruptly stopped on the page, halfway through the "1." Then it hit. I call them Zaps. They do different things sometimes, but there's a definite process that goes like this:

1. Bad thought
2. Terrible feeling or sensation like you just got attacked by a Dementor
3. Realization that you may die or go crazy or never be happy again if you don't do something fast

This time it went:

1. *There's something bad about that number.*

2. Tingling down neck and spine, stomach turns into overcooked Bavarian pretzel and hits shoes. *You will never be happy again for the rest of your life and you will think about it forever.*
3. Stop writing the number.

I don't know if that makes sense. It's like telling someone about a bad dream. They listen and they say "Oh, how terrible" but they don't really understand and they only half-care anyway because it wasn't real. And I think that's what people would say to me, but it is real. It's as real as anything. Think of the worst you have ever felt in your whole life—like if you got a bad flu or your dog died or you just got cut from a team you really wanted to be on—and imagine that happens when you take nine steps to the bathroom instead of ten. That's kind of what Zaps are like.

This wasn't a new thing. The Zaps happened, like, ten times a day—on some days, even more. I had no idea why, except for the logical reason that I was nuts. I didn't feel crazy, and I sincerely doubted that writing "19th" down on a certain line in my notebook was going to result in the end of the world. And yet I couldn't shake the feeling. I quickly scratched the number out.

"Why did you do that?" Max asked, glancing at me curiously.

I bit back a curse. I was extremely careful to hide the

Zaps, but I had lost focus for just a moment and had forgotten to check if Max was looking. My cheeks flushed.

"It was too messy," I said casually, avoiding his eyes. "Figured I'd miss the date."

Max snorted and went back to doodling. "Like you'd miss a test."

The rest of the class went by normally, with me stealing a few more looks at Raya.

Just before the day ended, the announcements crackled to life. The entire class jumped. Most had been either dozing off or talking quietly, as we had been given a work period to finish an assignment. I had already completed mine (which Max had copied), so we were talking about football. Well, Max was—I was just listening to him and thinking about how happy I was that there was no practice that night. Max was halfway through a story about a new route he had to run, when the principal's gruff voice cut in.

"Attention, classes. I have a quick announcement for the intermediates before the end of the day."

Principal Frost was not an overly happy guy. He looked like a cave troll and had a personality to match: dour and temperamental. Sometimes I wondered if he even went home after school, or if he just lived in his office surrounded by the piled bones of students who had gotten one too many detentions.

Principal Frost sounded even less thrilled than usual.

"As you may recall, our first annual Parent Council fund-raising dance will be happening two weeks from today," he said, sounding like the idea of a dance was making him nauseous. "Council has asked me to remind you to get your tickets now before they are sold out. Your teachers all have tickets available. Also, the noise in the hallways at the end of the day will not be tolerated. I will be walking around this afternoon handing out detentions. That is all. Oh, and clean your shoes off on the mats!"

With that, the announcement ended. The class instantly buzzed to life, with some of the girls looking excited and some of the guys making jokes or groaning. The principal had announced the dance at the beginning of the year, but I think everyone had kind of forgotten about it. Now my mind was racing. My eyes darted to Raya, who was of course looking completely oblivious to the news and listening distractedly to her friends. Was this my chance? Would anyone actually bring a date? I looked around. There certainly seemed to be a lot of whispering.

"This sounds lame," Max said.

"Agreed," I said, shifting a little and glancing at him. "But are you going to go?"

Max paused. "Probably."

Mr. Keats was shaking his head behind the desk, obviously realizing his assignment was long since forgotten.

The bell rang, and he just waved a hand. "Run along," he said. "Hand it in tomorrow."

Max and I quickly packed our stuff up and hurried out of the class. The conversations around us were still squarely focused on the dance. Taj, one of Max's football buddies, joined us, clapping Max on the shoulder and completely ignoring me. He did that a lot—probably because he was a foot taller and literally couldn't see me.

"You gonna ask someone to the dance?" Taj asked, grinning.

Max laughed. "I doubt it."

"No one is going to do that, right?" I chimed in.

"Why not?" Taj said. He was a big, burly kid who played linebacker. "I'm definitely going to. I don't want to be the kid sitting with you chumps while the rest of the boys are out there with the ladies."

"Ladies?" I asked, feeling my stomach flop over.

"An expression," Taj replied dryly. "Maxy, you need to ask someone. How about Clara?"

"She's a drama queen," Max said.

Taj winked. "And a hot one."

Max and Taj laughed while I hurried along beside them. So people *were* going to ask girls to the dance. Girls. Like Raya. Which meant I could theoretically ask her to go with me. I felt like I might vomit just thinking about it. Who was I kidding?

I was so preoccupied with the dance that I belatedly realized I was stepping on the tile cracks. There was no need to be reckless. I quickly adjusted my pace by three quarters so that my sneakers fell squarely on the dull white ceramic. I was a master of adjusting my stride so that no one would notice.

Up ahead a TA, Miss Lecky, was slowly walking down the hall, trailed by Sara Malvern. Sara was . . . different. She had gone to our school since preschool, but she was almost always taught separately from everyone else. She hadn't spoken once in all that time. Eight years, and not a word.

I still remembered the first day she joined a regular class. It was fifth grade, and when I walked in, she was sitting in the corner with a TA. Her eyes were on the board, and she didn't notice us walking in.

"Everyone say hi to Sara," my teacher, Mrs. Roberts, said before class.

We did, but Sara didn't even smile.

"Thank you," her TA said.

She didn't speak for weeks, of course. I saw her TA say things to her, but that was it. She just sat there and never responded.

It was November when she finally made a noise. She didn't talk. She screamed.

She looked off that day; flustered and sweaty and

fidgeting. She didn't usually fidget. I wasn't too far from her, so I saw it all. Her TA tried to calm her down, but it seemed to get worse. Finally I saw the TA try to grab her arm to calm her down. Sara screamed. The whole class jolted, and Mrs. Saunders dropped her chalk. Sara wrenched her hand away, pushed her desk over, and ran out into the hallway.

I never saw her in a regular class again.

I'm not sure if she could speak or if she had a learning disorder or what. Actually I had no idea what was wrong with her. Her big green eyes were always foggy and glazed over like she was looking at something far away. She didn't look at anyone or even seem to notice where she was. She just went through her day like a zombie, her mind elsewhere. She always wore a bracelet with a few little charms on it that jangled around as she walked, but I never saw what they were.

The other kids all called her Psycho Sara, but I had never seen her do anything crazy, besides that one time. She just seemed distracted. I could sympathize. Sometimes I felt pretty distracted myself.

Max, Taj, and I were just passing Sara when something unexpected happened.

She turned to me, her foggy eyes suddenly looking clear and sharp.

"Hello, Daniel," she said.

CHAPTER 2

I was so stunned, I didn't even have a chance to reply. Sara just continued shuffling down the hallway, and I turned and watched her go, Max and Taj slowing down beside me. Max looked at me in disbelief.

"Did Psycho Sara just talk to you?" he murmured.

I was watching her black ponytail bob away. "I think so."

Eight years. And she'd just said hello like we were old friends.

"That's weird," Taj said, starting down the hall. "Maybe she wants you to ask her to the dance."

Max broke out laughing and gave me a little push toward the front doors. "Let's go. You can ask her out tomorrow if you want."

I just laughed awkwardly and followed him out, but my

skin was still prickling everywhere like it was on fire. It was weird enough that she had talked to me. I hadn't thought she could even speak.

But what was worse was the strange feeling I'd gotten when she'd looked at me. It was like she was the only person who had ever *actually* seen me. But that was impossible. It didn't even make any sense.

Max and I stepped out into the cool fall air, and I tried to forget about Sara Malvern.

As I mentioned, I'm writing a book. I've been writing it for about a year now and once got to the twentieth page before deleting it all. It's supposed to be a masterpiece, but it doesn't feel like one. I like writing. It's just about the only time I don't get Zaps. I don't know if it's because my brain is too busy or because I get to create my own world where there aren't crazy people. Sometimes it's the only break I get in a day, and I think maybe it stops me from completely losing my mind.

Basically the book is about a kid named Daniel who wiped out the entire human race by accident and has to find a way to bring them back before the process becomes irreversible. His day starts like this:

When Daniel woke up, the velvety morning light was shining through his navy-blue curtains like on any other morning. But there was a heavy stillness in the air that unsettled him . . . a silence that was deeper and more ominous than normal. He quickly pulled on some worn jeans and a hoodie and hurried into the hallway, looking around curiously.

"Hello?" he called. His voice carried through the house like a frantic bat.

Daniel raced downstairs, but the kitchen was empty. It was eight thirty a.m. His family should have all been there: his mother, his brother, and his sister. He tried the TV. The radio. There was nothing but static.

Desperate, Daniel rushed into the street, fear clawing its way through his belly.

The streets were quiet. The houses watchful. There were no cars or pedestrians or noise of any kind carrying on the October breeze. He slowly walked into the middle of the street, the horrible, guilt-stricken realization flooding through him. He had done this. He had killed them all.

Out of the corner of his eye, he caught a glimpse of the moon, still reluctant to pass into the Earth. He froze, his eyes locked on the luminescent orb. His legs buckled and wavered.

The moon had changed since last night. It didn't seem possible, but there it was.

A part of it was missing.

I thought I would start with the action and jump backward, but I get indecisive. So I made a new plan, to just write the book and not change a single word until I have written the end. It's the only way I will ever finish.

I don't even know what I'm writing it for, since I have never showed my work to anyone and never plan to. Like I said, my writing is something I do for myself.

I didn't have too much time to dwell on Sara Malvern. After school Max and I played three hours of *Call of Duty* and ate two bags of potato chips, perched on the huge brown couches in my family room. My mom yelled at me for getting chips in the cushions twice. It was a typical Tuesday. I only had one Zap, this time in the bathroom with the light switch. I have a hard time with light switches—I don't know why.

Max decided to stay for dinner even after two bags of potato chips, because my mom was making chicken wings and she loves Max and always insists he stays. Max's dad left a few years ago, and his mom works really long hours, so he doesn't get a real dinner much. He's always happy to stick around. Max is one of those kids that is naturally comfortable around parents. He has a gift for polite conversation.

My brother and sister were there for dinner as well, but my dad didn't get home from work until late, so he always just ate leftovers wrapped in tinfoil and watched sports highlights.

"How was your day?" my mom asked Max, shoveling some salad onto my sister's plate.

We were gathered around the oak table. It had six seats because Max was at our house so much. The wood was marked with a thousand scratches and stains and nicks, but we'd gotten it from my grandma, and my mom liked it. She used really big placemats and center pieces to hide all the damage.

Max put down his wing. "Pretty good. They announced that school dance again."

"Lame," Steve said.

He thought everything was lame. Steve was sixteen and was way too cool for everyone—especially me. He played football and had a cheerleader girlfriend and wore baseball caps pretty much 24/7. We didn't look much alike. I was skinny with blue eyes, freckles, and hair that switched from blond to brown through the seasons. Steve was muscular and athletic, and his short dark hair matched unfriendly eyes. We didn't talk much. I would have liked to, but he wasn't as interested.

"That's not lame," my mother said, turning to me. "Are you going?"

I shrugged. "Maybe."

"You should," she said. "Max, make sure he does."

"Will do, Mrs. Leigh." Max winked at me. "He might even ask someone as a date."

I scowled, and my mom's eyes widened with delight.

"Really?" my mom asked. "Who is she?"

"No one," I muttered. I felt my cheeks burning.

My little sister, Emma, giggled. She was the opposite of Steve in just about every way. Emma was nine years old, supershy, and happiest when she was in her room reading. We were very close. She used to get me to sit by her bed and read to her every single night, and we still read together most nights.

Steve snorted and wolfed down a chicken wing. "Space Cadet isn't going to get a date."

My older brother called me Space Cadet too. And Über Nerd. Dink. Sally. Lame Wad. Pretty much everything but "Daniel," actually.

"That's not nice," my mother snarled. "Daniel is a catch."

I sighed. "Thanks, Mom."

"He is after a pretty popular girl," Max said. "I suggested someone else."

My mom looked concerned. "How popular?"

"Does it matter?" I asked, offended.

She hesitated. "It's just that popular girls can be so mean. I don't want you to get hurt."

Max laughed and sat back, rubbing his stomach tenderly. "He'll be fine. Thanks again, Mrs. Leigh. That was delicious. I should probably get going, though. I ate enough for the rest of the week."

"You want a ride?" she asked, already pushing her chair back.

"Na," he said. "Better walk this off. We got a game on Saturday, and I want to be ready."

I saw Max out, and he gave me a lopsided grin as he swung the front door open. He used that grin a lot when he knew people were mad at him. It usually worked, but I was still a bit sour.

"See you tomorrow, Space Cadet," he said with a casual salute.

"That was unnecessary."

He clapped me on the arm with a strong right hand and then started down the porch. "I know." He stopped and looked back, shooting me another lopsided grin. "By the way, I think you are a catch too."

"Shut up."

Max burst out laughing and hurried down the street, tucking his hands into his jean pockets. I scowled and shut the door, knowing my mom would definitely ask about Raya as soon as she got the chance. Heading upstairs to avoid any questions, I heard her fighting with Steve in the kitchen.

"I'm sixteen!" Steve shouted, banging his fist on the wall.

"You break that wall, you're paying for it!" my mom shrieked back. "And you're right, you're sixteen. It is a school night, and you will be home at ten!"

"That's not fair!"

They fought pretty much every night. Emma was already closing her bedroom door. I went to my room, opened my laptop, and checked my Facebook page. No updates.

Unable to resist, I opened Raya's page. She was smiling in her profile picture, instead of having one of those duck-faced selfies all the other popular girls had. I could never ask her out. She would say no, and then I couldn't have my dreams anymore.

I leaned back and looked around my room. It was a work in progress. One wall was covered in bookshelves and action figures, while the others had posters of bands and movies, and even one of Tom Brady that my dad had bought me when I'd made the football team. My desk was tucked under a dusty window that overlooked the street, and it was constantly littered with papers and drawings and books. I went to click on my home page, when I was Zapped. I went back and clicked it again. It still didn't feel right. I was at ten clicks and already feeling sweat bead on my forehead when I closed the browser. I could feel the urge to go back and try another click. But I knew it might start something that would take hours. I needed to write. Now.

Daniel stared at the moon in disbelief. It was like something had bitten the bottom right section, taking a chunk out like from a vanilla cookie. The moon stared back at him, glimmering faintly in the daylight.

A million thoughts ran through his head. But only one mattered. The device had worked. It had seemed so unlikely, tucked away in the attic and wrapped in a blanket of dust. But there was no other explanation. He had turned it on, and he had done something terrible.

As he stared in horror at the sky, something else caught his eye. A flicker of movement.

Daniel turned just in time to see something slip between two houses. Something big.

There was a gentle knock on my door, and an even softer voice. "Dan?"

"Come in."

Emma stepped inside, clutching a book under her arm and watching me from beneath a loose strand of blond hair.

"What are you doing?" she asked curiously, spying my laptop.

"Nothing," I said, shutting it before she could read anything. Even the little writing I had done had calmed me a bit. I didn't feel like I had to go click the link again, anyway. "What's up?"

She sat on the bed and shrugged. "You want to read for a while?"

"Sure."

We both lay down on the floor, staring up at the stucco ceiling. We did that a lot.

"What do you see?" she asked softly. Sometimes we created entire stories in the stucco. Her hair was splashed out like sand on the carpet.

I focused on one spot in particular. "A bird. An eagle maybe. Eroth, the King of Eagles, flying over the plains of Alog. He is preparing for a battle, I think. Goblins march on the kingdom. You?"

"A face. It looks like a girl. Pretty but cold eyes. A princess maybe . . . no . . . an archer. San'aa, the daughter of a fallen king, and the most famous archer in Arador. She can hit a bull's-eye from one hundred yards."

Emma looked over and smiled mischievously, her hazel eyes twinkling.

"Are you really going to ask a girl on a date?"

"Probably not."

She turned back to the ceiling. "You seemed different at dinner."

"How so?"

Emma seemed to think about that. "I don't know. Just . . . distant. Even more than usual."

That instantly brought Sara Malvern back to my mind. A tingle crept down my back and into my socks.

"Just tired, I guess," I replied, hoping she didn't hear the worry in my voice.

Emma opened her book and started reading. "I don't believe you."

"You never do."

We read until my mom came in and told Emma to go to bed. We both stood up, stretching sore limbs. Emma said good night and shuffled through my bedroom door. I watched her shadow turn the corner, fading into the hallway light. I was alone again.

I decided to write a bit more. As I opened my laptop, I noticed a piece of paper sticking out of one of the pockets of my backpack. Frowning, I picked it up. Scribbled in splotchy black ink was a note.

I need your help.
—Fellow Star Child

CHAPTER 3

I read the note several times and then folded it up with trembling hands. I had no idea what a Star Child was, or why anyone would possibly want my help. Someone must have snuck it into my bag when I wasn't looking.

But who?

I decided to look up "Star Child" first. Maybe that would give me some clues. My first search yielded this:

Star Children, according to a pseudoscientific New Age concept, are children who are believed to possess special, unusual, and sometimes supernatural traits or abilities.

I read through the first few articles. It sounded like conspiracy-theory stuff to me. Alien DNA, telepathic powers, and a lot of parents who believed their kids were Star Kids because they behaved badly.

I stayed up for a long time that night, checking Facebook for possible leads to the identity of the note leaver. Nobody had anything about Star Kids on their page, so I gave up and started getting ready for bed.

The Routine began at twelve thirty. It's something I have to do every night. I'll explain later. I went to sleep at four a.m.

The next day, I found Max in the school yard with the other cool kids. They just talked in the morning, though they usually played basketball or touch football at recess. That meant I had to play too, of course, even though I was even worse at basketball than I was at football. Max passed to me sometimes, but I usually passed it right back as quickly as possible and only shot when I was literally right under the net. The other guys gave me a hard time but let me play because of Max. If it wasn't for him, I would probably be in the corner reading with Emma, which I wouldn't have minded, except it would have made the prospect of talking to Raya even less likely.

As it was, Raya was actually in the circle of cool kids today, but by the time I got over there, the bell rang. She did give me a little smile, but that was it.

"Ready for the big game on Saturday?" Max asked me as we walked into class.

I sighed. "For the last time, I don't actually do anything."

"If the kicker gets hurt, we need you," he said seriously.

"How often does the kicker get hurt?"

Max paused. "Rarely. But still. And hey . . . you gonna ask her today?"

I snorted and pulled out my books. "Of course not."

"If you don't hurry, someone else will."

I thought about that for a moment and then shook my head. "I can't do it."

"You're a sissy."

"Agreed."

I was still thinking about Raya when Mr. Keats drawled, "Math books out, please." He looked like he wished he'd slept in today.

I sighed. That made two of us.

I don't like math for one important reason: the numbers.

We were doing some simple equations, and I kept having to change them. I made a four a forty-one. A nine a ninety-one. I didn't even write the six. Every time I saw a bad number, I had a Zap. A pit-of-my-stomach-things-are-wrong-do-something-now feeling. It was like being punched.

I tried to hide my notes from Max, but he noticed.

"Even I know that's wrong," he said, pointing at one answer. "Take the zero out, dufus."

"Oh, right," I muttered. But I didn't change it.

I started sweating profusely halfway through class—my skin hot and flushed and prickling. I changed so many numbers that it looked like code. Nine was giving me a real problem today.

Every time I wrote it, I felt like something bad was going to happen.

I don't know when it started or why, but some numbers are good, and some are not.

Here's my list:

1 = Okay
2 = Mostly okay
3 = Bad when combined with another three, four, five, or six
4 = Bad
5 = Okay
6 = Bad
7 = Mostly bad
8 = Always bad
9 = Bad
10 = Good

As you can imagine, it gets complicated in the double digits.

This probably sounds confusing, and that is likely because I might be crazy. But the numbers make me feel better or worse, and there is no arguing that. If I do something four times, my skin crawls and my stomach hurts and I can't breathe right. Five times, and I feel fine. The numbers control how many times I do things, but I also don't like writing or saying the numbers either. I know . . . bonkers.

But who am I to argue with feelings?

I don't know what triggers the Zaps, really. It's usually just a feeling or a thought that pops out of nowhere and attacks my brain and makes everything cold and dark and hopeless. I can be Zapped at any time, though thankfully, it's mostly at nighttime and when I'm alone. At those times it's relentless.

"I hate math," I muttered.

"Yeah," Max said. "And I hate that you aren't good at it. My grades are really suffering."

Max looked at me and frowned. "You all right?"

I wiped my head and forced a smiled. "Fine. Just a little warm in here, don't you think?"

"No."

"Oh. Maybe I'm sick."

Max put his hand on my forehead. "Yeah. Go dunk your head in water. You look like Raya just touched your arm or something."

"Thanks," I muttered.

"May I go to the bathroom?" I asked Mr. Keats.

I hurried down the hall, wiping my damp forehead and wondering what was wrong. Sometimes this happened at night, but never at school.

My arms and legs were tingling like they were on fire, and then they were numb and weak. I even started wondering if I was going to faint. Was I dying?

My breath caught. The hall started to spin.

I was almost to the bathroom when Sara Malvern walked out of the girls' bathroom. Miss Lecky was waiting for her in the hall, texting. Sara immediately turned to me and smiled.

"Hello, Daniel," she said.

I forced a smile. "Hi," I managed, trying to get to the bathroom.

She stepped in front of me.

"Splash a little water on your face," she said quietly. "It will pass."

Miss Lecky was watching us.

"Okay," I said.

Her eyes were doing it again . . . telling me that she knew exactly who I was and what I was seeing. But that was impossible. We had never spoken before yesterday. We had never even made eye contact.

Who was this girl?

I hurried to the bathroom and splashed some ice-cold water onto my cheeks, staring into the mirror and wondering what was happening to the pasty-faced kid looking back at me.

• • •

Things got better in last class. Way better. Mr. Keats assigned us a project about local government and said we could do it in groups of four. I immediately looked at Max, hoping he would find us two other partners quickly before the scramble began. The conversations and turning heads started quickly, but Mr. Keats was faster.

"I have already made the groups," he said, "so don't bother. Sometimes I think we only have one person doing the work of the group, so perhaps it will be a little more even if we mix it up."

He looked right at me. He would never put me with Max.

"Max, Clara, Brent, and Miguel," he began. "You can sit in the far corner."

"Super," Max muttered, eyeing Clara, who shot him a grin.

I rolled my eyes. "Poor you."

The groups were read out quickly, and I noticed very soon that my name had not yet been called, and neither had Raya's. A half hope, half panic started to form and was confirmed a minute later.

"Raya, Lisa, Daniel, and Tom. You can sit where Daniel is."

I probably had that deer-in-headlights look as Raya plopped down next to me and opened her notebook.

"Hey, Dan," she said warmly.

I put my arms under my desk to hide the spreading goose bumps. "Hey," I managed.

Lisa and Tom joined us. Lisa was a superquiet girl, and Tom was a football jock, so they just looked at each other awkwardly and remained silent. Clearly it was up to Raya to get the project moving.

"Anyone against town council?" she asked. "I figure we can get a quote that way—my mom knows one of the counselors."

"Sounds good," I said immediately.

"Whatever," Tom muttered.

"Okay," Lisa said, and then flushed, as if amazed that she had just spoken in front of Tom.

This would be fun.

Except it kind of was. We laid out what we were going to do and gave everyone homework, and Raya laughed twice. She has superwhite teeth. I needed to go brush.

Just before the bell Tom wandered off to talk with Taj, and Lisa went back to her desk, giving Raya and me an awkward smile and then scurrying away like a mouse. Raya shook her head.

"She'll get her work done, but we're probably going to have to cover for Tom."

"Yeah," I said. "I can do that."

She laughed. "I'm sure you can. You already do Max's work for him."

I opened my mouth to argue, and then stopped. "Yeah."

"Why?" she asked.

"He's my friend," I replied, shrugging. "It's no big deal."

"You should tell him to do his own work," she said. "He's smarter than he pretends. I think he likes to be a dumb jock because Taj and Tom are. He should be more like you."

I laughed. "Funny."

She raised an eyebrow. "What? I mean it."

"Max doesn't want to be like me," I said, still amazed that I was having a full conversation with Raya Singh. "He's a star football player and one of the most popular kids in school. And I'm . . . me."

"What's wrong with you?"

"I'm the backup kicker."

Raya snorted. "I didn't ask what position you play. What is with you boys and equating football to social status? I don't care if you're the backup water boy."

"I kind of am."

Raya laughed. "Of course you are. But the point is, you are smart, funny, and actually nice. I think that's a lot more important than being the backup kicker, don't you?"

I was dreaming again. I had to be.

"I guess," I said meekly. "And thanks."

"No problem. Unless you screw up this project, in which case, I'll kick your butt."

"Deal."

The bell rang, and for the first time ever, I wished it was broken. Raya rushed off, and I tried not to float off my chair after her. My entire body was tingling, but not with the feeling of dread. It was like a warm glow, as if I was out in the sun. When Max came back, I was smiling so much, he just laughed.

"How happy are you on a scale of one to ten right now?"

"Eleven."

"I figured. But wipe that grin off your face and get your cleats. We have practice."

The smile was gone in an instant. "Make that a two."

"You call that a push-up?" Coach Clemons yelled at me.

I was using my knees again. I couldn't help it. I couldn't do twenty push-ups.

"A type of push-up," I said hopefully.

"Lift those knees up, Leigh!" he blustered, spittle flying everywhere.

I did as I was told and face-planted into the grass. He sighed deeply and walked away.

"Laps!"

We ran for a while, which wasn't that bad, as it was a cold day. I usually spend most of my time sitting, and it can get chilly in football clothes.

"All right, Kevin," Coach Clemons said when we got back, "let's practice a few field goals."

Kevin was the starting kicker. He loved football almost as much as Max did. I trotted out with them, since I have to kick field goals too even if I am not officially invited.

I missed from the thirty and twenty-five. Coach Clemons just bit his lip.

"Go get the drinks ready, Leigh," he said eventually.

"Finally," I muttered, watching Max catch a pass with one hand.

"Nice one, Max!" Coach Clemons shouted.

I started arranging the cups of Gatorade and watched as Max continued running his routes. You'd think I would be jealous, but I wasn't really. I mean, it would have been nice to get some of his football skills, size, or general good looks, but I was at least happy that he was doing so well. When we were younger, we'd both been just social outcasts, and it was nice that he was becoming popular.

Part of me wondered if our friendship would survive high school when he was on the team there and had seniors to look cool in front of, but there wasn't much point worrying about it now. I hoped he would stick with me, but I knew things changed when you got older.

Just look at Steve. He used to be half-decent.

I arranged the Gatorades on the table in neat rows that were swiftly decimated on the first break. We actually did have a water boy for games, but it was my job in practice—though, last Saturday our water boy had had plans so I'd had to do it for the game too. I saw my dad watching as I filled cups in my Erie Hills Elephants uniform. When our eyes met, he quickly looked away.

But today Coach Clemons had different plans. I was sitting on the bench imagining a horde of goblins bursting through the chain-link fence at the end of the yard. I was right in the middle of snatching up a sword and charging, when Coach Clemons stepped in my way like a bulbous clipboard-wielding ogre.

"Leigh," he said. "Get out there. You look like a toothpick, so I'm assuming you can run. I want you to get down there as gunner and see if you can take down the returner. We're getting killed on that."

I looked up at him, frowning at his square-jawed grimace. "Did I do something wrong?"

The coach sighed. "Most kids want to play, son. Aren't you sick of the bench?"

"No. I quite like it."

"Go."

Sighing, I trotted out onto the field and took up position on the special teams unit. Max saw me and hurried over, looking alarmed. "You're playing?"

"Theoretically."

He patted my arm. "Go get 'em."

"Right."

I looked at the opposing line. Taj was there, eyeing me like I was a piece of beef jerky. Our returner, a superfast, stocky kid named Pete, was waiting at the far end of the field. I just had to run around the line, get down there, and tackle him. No problem. I fidgeted nervously, waiting for the snap.

I missed the bench already.

"Hut!" the punter shouted, and our long snapper tossed it back to him.

I took the long way around the line, just missing an arm bar from Taj. I really wasn't very fast, but I wasn't slow either. I made it around the defensive line and started for Pete, who was already positioning himself to get under the ball. I just ran as fast I could, grinning as I sprinted down the field. This wasn't so bad. As long as I didn't think about the actual hitting-anyone part, it was just like going for a run. Which I didn't do much, but that old lady across the street did, so how bad could it be? I didn't have time to worry out here. I just had to go hit a kid and try to get the football back. Simple.

I was ten feet away when Pete caught the ball. He pivoted, heading right and then left. I followed him, closing in fast. I couldn't really see much through the helmet, so I was just locked on Pete like a bloodhound. He started past me, and I turned to chase after him, still grinning. This was kind of fun.

I didn't see the impending collision until it was way too late.

There was a flash of a big, smiling Taj running at me for a block, and then it felt like I was hit by a truck. Suddenly I was flying through the air and wondering vaguely if Max would tell my family that I sort of played before I died. My dad would be happy. The ground hit just as hard as Taj, and I lay there, staring up at the afternoon sky. It was clear and blue. I smiled, but probably because I was concussed.

Max appeared over me. "You okay?"

"I don't think I want to play football anymore."

Max laughed. "Fair enough." He grabbed my hand. "Let's get you home. I think you're going to need some ice."

As we walked away, I saw Taj laughing. He was wearing number nine.

CHAPTER 4

Later that night I was lying on the couch eating pudding in the family room. Not because my jaw was broken or anything—I just liked chocolate pudding. Max had walked me home, and my mom had made a big fuss and waved her fingers across my eyes and inspected my skull for cracks. Then she'd just clucked and made me lie down.

When my dad got home, he walked in and said, "I heard you took a knock at football today. Were you playing?"

"Yeah," I said. "I was the gunner. Kind of got blocked and sent flying."

He smiled. "That's my boy. A few hits are good for you. Keep it up."

He went to put his briefcase away, and I frowned. Making my dad proud was painful.

I liked staying on the couch because it meant I could delay the Routine, but my mom wouldn't let me sleep down there. So at ten thirty I shuffled upstairs, exhausted.

She was going to check on me every two hours through the night in case I had a concussion. I wasn't going to get a lot of sleep. I changed into my sleep pants and started the Routine. I know most people call them pajama pants, but all I do is sleep in them, so it seems like a better name. I only had two hours before my first checkup, so I needed to start the Routine quickly.

Oh, you might be wondering what the Routine is. I've been doing it for five years. It grew out of a few different habits, and now it's permanent. There is no room for error. It looks like this:

1. Take ten steps from my bedroom to the bathroom
2. Brush my teeth with ten vertical movements on either side and five horizontal ones
3. Take five steps to the toilet
4. Pee, and then use two strips of toilet paper to wipe the rim in case I missed
5. Wash my hands with ten overlapping squeezes to either hand
6. Wipe hands on stupid pink doily towel—five squeezes to either hand
7. Take ten steps back to the bedroom

8. Flick lights on and off five times
9. Get to bed in five steps and climb into bed

As you can see, it's fairly simple. It might even be normal. I mean, how many times does anybody do anything when they walk the same distance or brush their teeth the same way? I just happen to know.

But that's not the problem. It rarely looks like that, because perfection is hard. I have to restart when I do it wrong, like if I take an extra step or pull off three strips of toilet paper instead of two or wash my hands nine times. I concentrate really hard, but sometimes I stumble or take four strips of toilet paper off by accident. And how do you accurately count hand washing?

Other times I just get Zapped out of nowhere, and then I have to do it again. It's all Zaps really; I think the Routine is just when the Zaps take over. Usually the fear is me thinking, *Do it again or you won't wake up in the morning,* and I keep doing it until I think I will wake up in the morning.

It was a particularly bad night. Since I was usually scared that I would die in my sleep if I did the Routine wrong, having a concussion and a real threat didn't exactly help. As a result the Routine looked like this:

1. Take ~~ten eleven~~ fifty steps from my bedroom to the bathroom

2. Brush my teeth with ~~ten~~ ~~eleven~~ . . . one hundred
    and ninety-two vertical movements on either side
    and ~~five~~ . . . three hundred horizontal ones
3. Take five steps to the toilet—and redo fifteen times
    and don't step on cracks
4. Pee, and then use ~~two~~ entire roll and replace roll and
    then use another roll and replace roll ~~strips~~ of toilet
    paper to wipe rim in case I missed
5. Wash my hands ~~with~~ ~~ten~~ twenty-fifty times and cry a
    little ~~overlapping~~ ~~squeezes~~ ~~to~~ ~~either~~ ~~hand~~
6. Wipe hands on stupid pink doily towel—~~five~~ one
    hundred squeezes to either hand
7. Take ten steps back to the bedroom—and redo
    twenty times
8. Flick lights on and off ~~five~~ three hundred and five
    times
9. Get to bed in five steps, feel bad, flick lights again,
    then redo light-flicking and steps one hundred times
    and climb into bed

When I finally finished the Routine, I lay in bed for a
long time, letting my silent tears soak back into my skin or
evaporate into tiny little hydrogen and oxygen particles that
would maybe get outside and rain on me tomorrow. That
thought made me relax. I like cycles. They are so much less
permanent than making a field goal or missing one.

That night I dreamed about Max and me watching TV. Except at one point Max looked at me and his eyes were totally black, like his pupils had taken over everything. Then he opened his mouth and his teeth were suddenly pointed fangs, and his features started to twist into something cruel and demonic, and I realized that it wasn't Max beside me at all. I woke up in the middle of the night sweating profusely.

Then I went to go flick the lights.

It was lunchtime. I had just missed a layup and was now standing dejectedly on the sidelines, as I had been "subbed out" by Taj, even though there was no one to take my place. I think "benched" would have been the more apt term, but there was no bench either, so finding the correct sports-themed colloquialism was difficult. I like the word "colloquialism." It's one of those inherently ironic words where it is the complete opposite of what it describes. I like words in general. They have established meanings but can vary, depending on how they're used or who uses them. They're like people—they're different depending on who's looking and how you read them.

For instance, Taj thinks I'm a useless nerd. Emma thinks I'm a clever older brother. Steve thinks I'm a Lame

Wad. My mom thinks I'm not cool enough to date Raya
Singh. Raya Singh thinks I'm . . .

Actually, I don't know what Raya thinks.

I immediately directed my attention to Raya. She
was standing with a group of girls by the washed-out
red bricks of the school, like she was on an indie rock
cover. I know what they look like because Raya likes
indie rock, and I did my research. She was also wearing a turquoise shawl and jean shorts, which I think was
considered retro chic according to *Cosmo*. I hoped she
asked if I liked them.

That's when something odd happened. Raya looked
at me and waved.

The other girls followed her gaze and all shared some
sort of similar reaction, like confusion, scandal, and bewil-
derment. Ashley Peters was looking behind me in case
someone cool was hiding there. It felt like someone was
putting a blowtorch to my cheeks, but I managed a smile
and a wave.

The girls quickly turned back to Raya and started
talking. What had just happened?

I stood there for a moment, pondering. And then
Raya started walking toward me.

Now I would have to say something. My brain was spinning.

"Hey, Daniel," she said warmly.

"Hi," I replied. It was the best I could do on such short notice.

She raised an eyebrow. "Are you the coach, or what?"

"More like the reporter," I said. "I was going to do the postgame interviews."

She laughed. "Listen, my mom talked to her friend, that town counselor I told you about, and we just need to pop into his office next week. Are you free after school? It's just on First Street. My mom can drive."

"Yeah, definitely," I said. "Anytime. I mean, other than—"

"Mondays, Wednesdays, and Thursdays," she replied dryly. "We wouldn't want you to miss that sport that you hate playing."

"Exactly," I said.

She hesitated. Why was she hesitating? Was this my chance? *Think, Daniel!*

I opened my mouth, but she beat me to it.

"Do you know what Max's deal is?"

It was like being kicked in the stomach by a mule. It felt like a Zap almost, but this wasn't the kind I could fix. This was the kind that just happened because life is full of mule kicks to the stomach.

"In what sense?" I asked meekly.

"In the sense of, does he like anyone?" Raya asked. Her

eyes followed him as he played basketball. "Is he going to the dance?"

"Yeah," I said. "I think so. He hasn't asked anyone, though, if that's what you're wondering."

She smiled. My stomach felt bruised. Would Max ask her out now?

"Clara has been freaking out," Raya said. "She really likes him, as I'm sure you know. I can finally tell her he's not taking some girl from another school or something. Can you tell him to just ask her and get it over with so she stops bothering me? I feel like a loser asking you in the first place, but she made me."

My bruised stomach suddenly felt cured. She didn't like Max.

"Yeah, I know," I said. "I'll tell him. Otherwise he's stuck with me as a date, and I don't look nearly as good in a dress."

She laughed. "I don't know . . . you've got the girly figure. See you in class."

She turned to go. This was my only chance. *Just ask.*

But the words failed me, just for a moment. It was too long.

"Raya!" someone called out.

I turned to see the sweating, lumbering Taj close in on her.

"You wanna go to the dance?" he asked.

Was it my imagination, or did her eyes dart to me for just a split second?

"Yeah," she said, sounding less than enthused, "sure."

"Great," Taj said. "See you later."

Then he was playing basketball again. Raya was walking away.

And I was standing on the sidelines, wondering if anyone would notice if I went home.

CHAPTER 5

All I will tell you about my Routine that night is that I was at 437 light switch flicks when I finally went to bed. From the street, it probably looked like a dance party.

When I finally completed the Routine, I lay there thinking about Raya.

Let me describe the feeling of heartache, in case you don't know:

1. Your mind says you messed up and nobody likes you and the other person is too good for you.
2. Then your mind says you will never be happy because happiness is related to that other person liking you and they don't, so of course you are never going to be happy again.

3. Then your mind says you don't control your own happiness and that is scary.
4. Then your stomach starts to hurt, you don't breathe right, your arms tingle, your head hurts, and you can't go to sleep.
5. Then you curl into a ball because there's nothing else you can do.

Now let me describe the feeling of being Zapped:

1. Your mind says you messed up and did something wrong.
2. Then your mind says you will never be happy because happiness is related to that thing you did wrong, and if you don't fix it, you will never be happy again.
3. Then your mind says you don't control your own happiness and that is scary.
4. Then your stomach starts to hurt, you don't breathe right, your arms tingle, your head hurts, and you can't go to sleep.
5. Then you realize you can fix the thing you messed up, and you cry a little because it doesn't make any sense, but then you fix it because there's nothing else you can do. But then you feel worse because it didn't make any sense, so you curl up because nothing makes any sense anymore.

Being Zapped is kind of like heartache. Except heartache doesn't also mean that I think I might die or my little sister might die or I might destroy the entire world if I don't fix the problem.

I guess being Zapped is worse. But I still wish I had asked Raya to the dance.

School was a little awkward for the next week. Raya and I were still working on the project, and the next week we went to the counselor's office with Lisa. Tom said he was busy. We got a quote that said:

> *"Municipal government may not be the most romantic branch of government, but it's the one that affects your daily life the most. We make the decisions on local taxes, garbage pickup, and the stoplights that keep this great town moving. We also have an election coming up, so tell your parents to vote for Steve Bradley."*

It felt like an authentic politician quote. Raya did most of the talking during our actual presentation, which was two days later. Lisa said "Any questions?" really quietly, and I talked a little bit about the election process, which nobody listened to except Mr. Keats. Tom just stood there and smirked a lot and made faces with the other football players, but he still got an A. Group work.

After that presentation Raya and I congratulated each other.

"It was nice working with somebody who actually knows what 'municipal' means," she said.

I smiled. "Same to you."

The bell had rung, and we were packing our things.

"So, you going to the dance on Tuesday?" she asked. "It feels so weird to say that. I don't know why we have to have our dances on weekdays. Well, yes I do, actually. Mr. Frost is evil."

It was Friday, and the dance was all anyone was talking about.

I shrugged. "I don't know. Maybe. Max never asked Clara, so I guess we might go."

"You should. It's going to be lame, and I need someone to share witty observations with."

I looked at her hopefully.

"I can do that," I said.

She laughed. "I know you can. Have a good weekend, Dan."

"You too," I said, grinning.

My week was actually pretty good, now that I thought about it.

We went to Sushi King for dinner that night. Even Steve came. I was eating unagi, which is eel. I find them interesting because eels are not at all aesthetically pleasing and everyone says that, but is a cow?

"Emma got a ninety-five on her math test yesterday," my mom said.

My dad glanced at Emma. "Oh?"

"Yeah," Emma said. "Missed an easy one."

My dad adjusted his glasses.

He smiled at Emma. "Well, ninety-five is pretty good," he said. "But I'm sure you'll get a hundred next time."

Steve snorted. "I got a sixty-two on my last math test."

My mother sighed. "I was going to save that news for later."

"Better than a fail," my dad said. He always said things like that to Steve.

"If I didn't have two brains for siblings—" Steve said.

"That's enough," my mother said curtly. "How is your tuna, Emma?"

"Good, thank you," she replied. She always picked her sushi apart before she ate it.

"And how is everything with you, Daniel?" my mom asked.

I shrugged. "Good."

"How's the team looking?" my dad asked. Football was really the only thing he talked about other than grades and chores. I think he liked football more than he liked me.

"Not bad," I said. "We make the play-offs if we win this weekend."

He grinned. "I know. I think you could go for a run. Max is really playing well."

"Don't forget about Daniel's water organizing," Steve said.

My dad forced a smile. "He is a part of the team. It's a team sport."

"Thanks, Dad," I muttered, turning back to my sushi. I bit into a piece of salmon. "I try."

"Not with your mouth full," my mom said sharply. "Steve, eat your dinner."

"This salmon is gross," Steve said, pushing it away. "I told you we should just go to McDonald's."

"Don't waste food," my dad said quietly.

Steve paused, and then he finished his salmon.

"Hut!"

Tom Dernt dropped back, cocking his arm and scanning the field. The offensive line held strong, pushing back the scrambling Halton Hawks and grunting and straining as their helmets smashed together.

Tom paused for a moment, waiting for an opening. Just then one of the Hawks broke through the line, sidestepping the block and closing in. A gasp went through the crowd. But Tom was faster.

He released the ball just as he was hit, and the pigskin floated through the air, spinning gently.

It was almost silent as it passed under the morning sky.

And then it dropped right into Max's outstretched hands, and he sprinted into the end zone—with a couple of minutes left, that was the clincher.

The entire stadium went mad. It was a fifteen-point lead.

I watched as the crowd celebrated—even Raya was there. Clara was going nuts beside her.

My parents were watching, clapping and cheering, and I saw my dad glance at me and then quickly look away again. I hadn't even been on the field once, of course. Max was enveloped with hugs. Raya watched as he and Taj high-fived on the field. Of course she was smiling.

She was going to the dance with a real football player.

I just sighed and poured some more Gatorade. Our water boy was away again this weekend—apparently he had quite the social life. I arranged the cups in small tri-angles, with two-inch gaps to avoid spillage, and then gave Max a clap on the shoulder as he came for a drink.

"Nice catch," I said.

"Thanks, man," he said, grinning. "Left me wide open. Play-offs, baby."

I was going to say something else, but he crumpled his cup and threw it toward the garbage, where it joined the missed shots on the grass. Without another word he was gone, talking to Coach.

I went to pick up the cups. I hate littering. As I dropped them into the garbage, I caught a glimpse of my dad watching me again. He forced a smile and turned away.

I realized if I was ever going to get Raya Singh to go out with me, I needed to step my game up. Regardless of what she said, I was still the backup kicker, seemingly starting water boy, and the janitor.

I needed advice on how to win her over. And there was only one person to turn to.

Steve looked at me like I had finally lost it.

"You want me to do what?" he asked, slowly taking off his headphones.

I shifted uncomfortably. "I just need advice. On how to impress girls."

"Do I look like a dating coach?" he snarled.

"Maybe?" I said. "Not sure what they would look like."

"Get out."

I slumped. "But—"

"Go."

Dejected, I turned and started for the door, wondering what I was going to do now. I heard a protracted sigh behind me. "Wait."

He took his headphones off again and leaned back in his chair, eyeing me critically.

"Do you want me to start with the physical changes or the personality?"

"Uh . . ."

He nodded. "We'll do both. First of all, as I have repeatedly noted throughout your life, you look like a used Q-tip. It's not just the toothpick arms. It's the blond hair that hangs over your ears like wax."

I self-consciously put my hands over my ears. Maybe I could use a trim. Steve stroked his chin like an evil dictator. His ball cap was perched low, almost to his nose.

"So start with some biceps curls and push-ups. A haircut. And try to suck less at football, will you?" He waved a hand dismissively. "This is all long term, though. When is the dance?"

"Tuesday," I murmured.

He snorted. "Great. All right. I'm going to give you some quick advice here. Women dig confidence. Stop shuffling around in Max's shadow. Stand out a little, you know? Play to your strengths."

"What are those?"

Steve scowled and turned back to his computer. "Get lost." He paused. "You're smart. Stop trying to be a football player, because you stink at it. Or just give up, because if she's popular, she probably won't date you anyway. Your choice."

"Thanks," I said, meaning it. He had called me smart. That was definite progress.

"Yeah, yeah," he muttered. "Close my door, Lame Wad."

I left him alone and went back to my room, thinking about what he had said. I sat down at my computer and prepared to start writing. That was when I noticed I had an email from the address stillwaiting@email.com. It read:

> *We are running out of time.*
> *—Fellow Star Child*

I stared at the email for a while and then responded: *Who are you?* and waited. It only took a minute.

> *If you don't know, you can't help me.*

CHAPTER 6

Everyone was talking about two things: the game and the dance. Taj was strutting around like a rooster, and Max was having a full day of back pats and "great game," even from the teachers. I was even more invisible than usual, which I knew from Steve was a problem.

I needed more visibility.

At lunch everyone was huddled together talking about the dance. It was my chance to talk to Raya. I squeezed in next to her at the big lunch table. Taj was busy reliving the game with Max.

"Hey," I said.

She smiled. "Hey."

The cafeteria was an ugly old room with stained tiles and rows of crowded benches. It always smelled like tuna sandwiches, probably because Kevin ate one every day. It was also the noisiest place I have ever been, and I had to raise my voice just to talk to Raya right next to me.

"All ready for the big dance?"

She rolled her eyes. "If I have to talk about it one more time, I'm changing schools."

I laughed. "Agreed. I saw you at the game on Saturday. You don't usually come."

"I know," she said. "I went against my better judgment. Taj asked."

I stiffened just a little, my eyes flicking over to him. "Makes sense."

We were silent for a moment.

"You did a nice job with the Gatorade."

"Thank you," I said. "It's an art form, you know. Most important job by far."

Raya giggled, shaking her head. "Naturally. You'll be critical in the play-offs."

Why was I talking about football again? I thought back to Steve's advice—be smart.

"So," I said, "what do you think about the new policy on Iran? A bit pragmatic, right?"

She frowned. "Where did that come from?"

"I don't know," I said. "I just thought you would be interested. Not really anyone I can talk to about that stuff, you know? You seemed like you would know about it."

"I'm not Iranian," she said, sounding a bit terse. "I'm Indian."

"I know . . . I just meant . . ."

She forced a smile. "No big deal. Not too into politics. Clara, what are you doing?"

She turned away, launching into conversation with Clara about her jeans.

That had gone well.

"So your mom is going to grab me at seven?" Max asked during history. It was the Tuesday of the dance.

"Yeah," I replied. "But you know it starts at seven, right?"

He snorted. "Do you really want to be there on time?"

"No?" I guessed.

"Of course not. I'd go even later, but it's only two hours long anyway."

Mr. Keats was talking in the background about the Constitution. No one was listening. I saw Clara looking over at Max hopefully. She had turned down, like, five invitations already in the hopes that Max would still ask her. She looked like a Barbie doll today. Her hair was in elaborate curls, and her skin looked oddly smooth and shiny.

Max noticed her and looked away.

"Are you going to dance with her tonight?" I asked.

He shrugged. "Maybe. We'll see how it goes."

I had to ask. "Do you really not like her? I mean, she's vapid, crass, and sardonic—"

Max raised his eyebrows.

"She's mean," I said. "But she's also pretty."

Max looked uncomfortable. He did that sometimes when I talked about Clara.

"Yeah, she's cute," he agreed. "But she's just not my type. Like you said . . . she's mean."

"Not to you."

He looked at me. "And has she ever said two words to you?"

"Yeah," I said. "'Where's Max?'"

He snorted and turned back to the board. "We'll see. Are you wearing anything nice?"

"Dress pants and a collared shirt," I said, suddenly alarmed that we hadn't discussed this yet. "Are you wearing jeans or something?"

"Mom wouldn't let me. Try not to wear a blue shirt. We don't need to be dates and twins."

"Right." On to my second shirt choice.

As we were leaving school that afternoon, Clara delayed extra long, and Max just walked right by her. Raya gave me a little smile, and then I saw Taj give her a little smile, and I quickly turned away.

"See you tonight, Space Cadet," Max said.

"See ya," I said, heading off to find Emma.

It was a Tuesday. It had to be a good day, right?

It takes me a long time to get ready for events. Today I actually had to think about my outfit, so it was not helping.

I had cosmopolitan.com opened on my computer, along with, at least five men's style sites.

I stared in the mirror, turning right and left and eyeing my reflection carefully. Blue was definitely my color. It matched my eyes, and cosmopolitan.com said the eyes were the most important thing to girls. But Max had already called it. I grimaced and took off the blue shirt, flipping through my closet.

I only had five dress shirts, and three were blue. There was also one black and one taupe.

Checking the men's fashion sites, I saw that black wasn't really in style. There was nothing about taupe. I tried both shirts on ten times and then finally settled on taupe. It was fabulously neutral.

My mom inspected me before I left. She fixed my hair with nervous hands.

"You need a trim," she said, tucking my tufts of blond hair behind my ears. "Are you sleeping all right? You look sick. It's those circles under your eyes. And you're so pale. You look like a ghost."

"This isn't helping."

She stepped back and smiled. "But you're still so handsome. You sure you won't wear blue?"

"Yes."

She sighed. "Fine. Let's go."

She gave me pointers the entire way there. "Girls like p's and q's, no matter what they say. Being polite goes a long way," she said. "You have to dance. Girls love a dancer. They don't like the guy in the corner." She looked at me sternly.

"And remember. The quiet girls in the corner probably want to dance too. Don't always go after the pretty ones."

This was all fairly horrifying, of course, so I just sat there silently. We picked up Max, and as he was walking toward the car, she turned to me and said, "See how good he looks in blue?"

I sighed.

"Hey, Mrs. Leigh," he said, jumping into the car. "Daniel, love the color."

We pulled up in front of the school, and my mom looked at me.

"Have fun, you two. You sure your mom is okay to pick you guys up?"

"Yeah," Max said. "She can't wait to ask me all about it."

My mom laughed. "I'm sure. Now get in there. You're late."

We piled out and walked inside. School is weird at night. It's exciting for some reason, since I always think it just doesn't exist when we're not in class.

We reached the gym, handed in our tickets, and walked inside.

That's when it all went wrong.

CHAPTER 7

I'm not sure I like the idea of fate. It kind of means you don't have a choice. Or you can make choices, but they'll still bring you to the same place. I like the idea of choice, because I don't get to do it much. Once I tried to not brush my teeth the correct amount of times. And most people would probably say that was an easy thing to do, but for me it was like lying down on some train tracks waiting for a train to hit me, and I heard it rumble and I knew I could get up, and so I did, because why would I want to be hit by a train? So of course I brushed my teeth and went to bed.

The dance looked like fun. It was in the gym, but it was dark enough that everyone kind of looked the same, and there were lights set up, flitting around like multicolored birds. The music was loud and a few people were even dancing. One of them was Mrs. Lenner, who was really loud and wore a lot of yellow and orange outfits.

Principal Frost was watching in the corner, looking agitated.

I looked around, and saw that Raya was there already. She looked beautiful.

She was wearing a dress. I didn't think she wore dresses. Hers was purple. Her hair was tied back, and I think she had lip gloss on or something, because her lips sparkled.

"Raya looks good," Max said, sounding bemused.

"Yeah," I managed.

"Pull it together, Space Cadet," he said. "Let's go find the guys."

I followed him, but my eyes didn't. They were locked on Raya. I never realized how much I liked the color purple.

Raya saw me and smiled. I smiled and then quickly turned away. I was glad it was dark.

"What up, Max?" Taj said, wearing a white dress shirt that was way too small.

How did he have so many muscles?

"You know," Max said, standing beside him and looking out at the crowd. "Good crowd."

Taj nudged Max. "Check out Clara."

We both looked. Even I was impressed.

Her blond ringlets spilled all the way down her back and over a sky-blue dress.

"Wow," I said.

"Wow indeed," Max replied, giving her a little wave. "I didn't know this was the prom."

Taj snorted. "You should go talk to her."

"Maybe later," he said. "Let's go join the group."

"I'll catch up," Taj said. "Tom and I are working on a little routine. 'Billie Jean,' baby."

Max laughed and shook his head. "I can hardly wait."

I felt my cheeks getting even hotter as we got closer to Raya. She was standing with Ashley, and Clara appeared almost instantly, flashing her gleaming white teeth.

"Hey, Max," she said. "Love the shirt."

He smiled. "You look nice. Like a princess or something."

I thought she was going to faint, she looked so happy. "It's just a thing I had in the closet."

"Hey, Dan," Raya said. "Love your shirt too."

Max smirked. I fixed my collar. "Just a thing I had in my dad's closet."

Clara gave me an annoyed look and then walked right past me to talk to Max, laughing at a joke he hadn't even told yet. I stepped a bit closer to Raya to get out of her way.

"Hey," I said nervously. "I just wanted to apologize—"

"No," she said. "I need to apologize. I was being stupid. I'm just, like . . . the only Indian girl in the school, and I get a little sensitive sometimes. We're good."

"Good," I said. "Having fun yet?"

Raya rolled her eyes. "The best. Loud music and boys staring at me across the gym like I might attack them. I do like watching Mrs. Lenner dance, though. That will probably be the highlight of my night."

"If our dates don't stop clowning around," Ashley agreed, who was Tom's date. "I'm going to go see if that dufus plans on coming over here tonight or just dancing in the corner with his boyfriend."

She stormed off, leaving me with Raya. I loved dances. Everyone was so preoccupied.

"So how's your date going?" she asked me, looking at Max.

"Pretty good," I said. "I mean, my mom picked him up, and I forgot a corsage, so not great."

She giggled. "Better than mine. Taj's older brother picked us up in a Camaro and told him to have fun while winking at me. It almost made me vomit."

"That would have been bad for the Camaro."

"I know. So did your mom comb your hair for you?"

I paused. "She fixed it. I did most of the original combing."

She reached over and messed it up a little. The touch sent shivers right down to my feet.

"Too much combing. I like it like you haven't slept in a week because you were writing a novel."

I glanced at her. "How do you know I like to write?"

"Because you do it sometimes when no one is looking." She smiled. "Or so you thought."

This was the greatest conversation of my life. Clara and Max rejoined the group, but my arms didn't stop tingling for a second. We stood there and talked until Clara pulled Raya away to the bathroom.

"How happy?" Max asked.

"Twelve."

"I thought so." He watched Clara disappear into the bathroom. "She wants to dance."

"So dance."

He looked at me. "I don't like her."

"She looks like Cinderella."

"And she talks like the evil stepmother."

I snorted. "So don't marry her. Just dance with her and act like Prince Charming."

"And if she wants to go out or something?"

"Disappear at midnight."

He sighed and turned to the bathroom. "Yeah."

"Buck up," I said. "And I need to go to the bathroom too. I drank five pops before I came."

"Why?" he asked, laughing.

"Nervous drinker," I replied. "I'll be back."

I hurried off to the bathroom, practically gliding across the gym. Raya had talked to me and touched my hair. She knew I liked to write. She'd said she liked my hair messy.

My brain was so busy, it didn't even worry about the lines of the floor. I stepped on the half-court line. I never step on the half-court line. It's red and highly ominous.

I was almost to the bathroom when I saw Sara sitting at a table. Miss Lecky was beside her. Sara's dark hair was curled, and she was wearing a green blouse and dress pants. She was just sitting there, her eyes glazed over while Miss Lecky texted. Maybe Sara's parents thought it was good for her to get out.

We met eyes for a moment, but she didn't say anything this time. She just watched me.

It was unnerving, and I felt her eyes on me all the way to the bathroom. But when I turned back, she was staring at nothing again, the bright lights playing tricks on her face. I wondered where her mind went when she stared.

I guess I took a long time. I was nervous, so it took me a while to pee, and then I fixed my hair for five minutes to try to make it look messy, which I know is ironic, but there are certain types of messy. When I was finally satisfied that I looked like an exhausted writer, I emerged from the bathroom.

I stopped.

Raya was on the dance floor with Taj. Obviously Ashley had succeeded in getting the two boys to pay attention to them, because she was dancing with Tom as well. That was one thing, but Raya was having fun. She was laughing and letting Taj put his arm around her back, and then they were dancing close and then doing something like the funky chicken, and then they were close again.

I'd never seen her laugh like that. When she laughed with me it was quiet, smart laughter. I'd thought that was her laugh. But this was different. It was fun and loud. I felt the heartache again. *You're not good enough. You messed up.* My stomach started to hurt, my breathing didn't feel right, my skin went cold. I looked for Max, but he was dancing with Clara.

I was alone.

I found my way to a table in the corner of the gym. There were bowls of chips on them all. I sat at a table by myself, and then I felt a Zap. I moved the chip bowl. Then I tapped my leg. Then I started to cross my legs. I moved the chip bowl again. The Zaps grew stronger.

You moved the chip bowl wrong. You're going to feel like this forever. Raya is never going to like you because you're crazy. You need to move the chip bowl.

My stomach hurt. My hands were cold. I wanted to run away.

You tapped wrong. Your stomach hurts because you are dying. Now your chest hurts. You are going to die if you don't tap again. Now you need to go home. But you have to tap first. Not eight times. Not nine. Ten. No, that didn't feel right. Back to one. No. Two. No. Three.

I felt the sweat forming on my brow. When I get into these Zap modes, it's hard to think or feel or do anything but try to save myself from the fear. I stood up, sweat pouring down my face.

I wasn't having fun anymore. I didn't want to be there.

I started for the gym door. Sara was watching me again. Now she was interested.

I counted my steps. I avoided the lines. I skipped tables and didn't make eye contact. My entire body was on fire and ice cold and I couldn't breathe right. My chest hurt. My head hurt. I was dying.

"Daniel!" someone called.

I looked back, and Raya was walking toward me. I wanted to smile and say something clever, but I couldn't.

"Where are you going?" she asked.

I only kind of heard her. "Home," I managed. "I don't feel very good."

I tried to get away, but she caught my arm. She looked concerned.

"You're sweating."

I pulled my arm away. "I know. The food or something."

"You seemed fine—"

"It happened fast," I said. She seemed so far away. I was disconnecting. The Great Space was here.

"Are you sure?" she said. "Why don't you just stick around—"

"Sorry," I replied, starting for the door. I was leaving her behind me. Raya Singh. But she was so far away anyway. I couldn't feel anymore. I was passing the door when I saw the switch. *Zap.*

1. *You will never escape the Great Space unless you switch it.*
2. *The Great Space is even worse than usual. I can't feel. I can't think. I'm drifting away. My chest hurts and I'm going to die. I want to be normal again. I want to go home.*
3. *Flick the switch, and you will feel better.*

My rational brain tried to flick on again. I knew the light switch meant nothing. I could leave it and go home, and nothing would change. But then my rational brain started to fade again, and I couldn't think about anything except that I was going to die. And I didn't want to die. I had to fix this.

And then, to my horror, I flicked the switch. The lights came on, and everyone looked up. I didn't really see them, but I saw Sara. She was smiling.

I flicked the lights off again. Everyone was staring at me.

Raya looked confused.

I ran out of the school. Literally ran. I didn't stop until I was far from the school and Max wouldn't be able to find me. I walked home in the darkness, my hands in my pockets, tears streaming down my face. I was still in the Great Space, but this time I could feel fear.

Real fear.

I had just flicked the lights in front of the entire school. I had lost my last bit of control.

My fear started to turn to anger. I didn't want to go home and do the Routine. I didn't want to spend three hours getting into bed. I just wanted to be like Max and Taj and the other kids.

I didn't want to be crazy.

When I got home, I snuck inside. My dad was in the basement, and my mom was watching TV in her bedroom. The house was quiet. I slipped off my shoes, my cheeks still hot with tears. I was furious.

I wanted desperately to skip the Routine, but I couldn't. I ended up walking back and forth to the bathroom for one hundred and forty-nine steps, shouting silent pleas and shaking and trying to go to bed before I turned back and did it again. When I heard my mom stirring, I finally made it to the bathroom, and I brushed my teeth until my gums were bleeding, and kept going until the toothpaste was red. My hands were shaking, but I couldn't stop. If I stopped, I was going to die. I wasn't going to wake up. I used two rolls of toilet paper and clogged the toilet, and I felt my face twisting and tears spilling as I used the plunger. I washed my hands until they were pink and it felt like the skin was peeling off. I heard more movement in my parents' room and stopped, and then I hurried back to my room and flicked the lights. My face was sopping wet with sweat and tears. Sometimes I thought I didn't want to wake up anyway, and then I got scared and I flicked the switch again. It took me hours. I cried the whole time, my body racked with pain, and I would scream out in silence and fall on my knees and sometimes think I couldn't do it anymore. That it would be easier to be gone. But I was afraid of death. I was afraid of everything.

I did the whole Routine in perfect silence. When my dad went to bed, I turned the lights off and climbed into bed. He poked his head inside.

"How was the dance?" he asked.

"Okay," I said. I had the blanket over my face. I couldn't let him see me.

He hesitated. "I heard you walking around a bit. Everything all right?"

I was glad the blanket was covering my face. "Yeah. Sorry. Just . . . had a bit of a stomach thing. I feel fine now."

"Good," he said, sounding unconvinced. "Well, get some sleep. We can talk in the morning."

When the bedroom door closed, I started again. I flicked the light switch until my hand was numb. I couldn't fix it. The numbers were wrong. Everything was wrong.

Of course I could never date Raya. Not because I was the backup kicker or had toothpick arms.

I could never date her, because I was crazy. And I was afraid.

I lay in bed until my eyes grew heavy and the darkness took me.

CHAPTER 8

The mornings are usually my favorite time of the day. I feel fresh. The Great Space is usually gone, and for a few seconds I am too tired to think about Zaps. It's almost peaceful. But today I woke up and wished for the sun to go away. I wasn't ready to go back to school. I didn't want to face the other kids after last night. It was Halloween, which I had almost forgotten. Some kids would be dressed up at school—maybe I could wear a mask. But they don't let you wear masks to school. That would be too convenient.

I lay there for a while, thinking about my book. Today I wanted to wake up and be the only human on earth.

I wondered if a part of me had always wanted that.

After rolling out of bed, I pulled on a hoodie and some faded jeans, shoved my hands into my pockets, and went downstairs. It was already one of those mornings where it feels like you ate something rotten. It twists around in your gut like a pack of eels. And not the unagi kind.

Emma was waiting at the table, eating alone and reading the paper. She was the only nine-year-old I knew who read the paper. She put it down and flashed me a smile. She wasn't dressed up either. She didn't usually participate in what she called "commercial holidays."

"How was it?" she asked eagerly.

"Okay," I murmured, pouring some cereal.

She watched me until I sat down. "You're lying. What happened?"

"Nothing."

"Did you kiss Raya?"

"No."

"Did you try to dance and humiliate yourself?"

I scowled. "I didn't dance."

"But you did humiliate yourself."

I thought about that for a moment, and then dug into my cereal. "Maybe."

"There's a surprise," Steve chimed in, shuffling into the kitchen. He grabbed a protein drink. "Did you try to dance?"

I put my spoon down. "Why does everyone assume that would humiliate me?"

Steve took a gulp and stared at me. "Was it to do with that girl?"

"Yes."

He exchanged a knowing look with Emma. "She was with someone else."

"Yeah," I muttered. "But I knew that before. I just didn't . . . expect her to be so happy."

Emma frowned. "Isn't that the point of a dance?"

Steve took another drink, and then gave me a rare pat on the shoulder. "Buck up. No one likes a mope."

With that, he disappeared upstairs, and I just sighed and looked at Emma.

"He should be a psychologist."

Max hurried over as soon as I got into the yard. He looked concerned.

"What happened to you last night? I texted but . . ."

I shrugged, trying to look casual. "Just wasn't feeling too well. No big deal. How was the rest of the night?"

Max seemed dubious, but he cracked a grin. "Pretty good. Taj and Tom did a full dance routine."

"I bet that was a hit," I said darkly.

Max obviously caught the shift in tone. He glanced back at the group, where Raya was talking with Clara. Both of them still had their hair nicely done but were back in their normal clothes. It seemed that none of the eighth graders had dressed up. I was glad I hadn't worn my Luke Skywalker costume.

"She isn't dating him or anything."

"Doesn't matter," I said. "She likes him. And let's be honest—she would never like me."

"Why not?"

I rolled my eyes. "Because I'm me. A nobody. My brother's right. I look like a used Q-tip."

Max snorted. "That's pretty good."

"Yeah," I said, turning for the doors. "I have to use the bathroom."

"I'm kidding," Max said.

"It's cool. I just need to pee."

"Dan?"

I looked back, and Max fidgeted a little, obviously uncomfortable.

"What was with the light thing?"

I paused. "I thought I'd dropped something. Was just having a quick look."

"Oh," he said. "Cool. I'll see you in class."

"Yeah."

I left him there and went inside, feeling my eyes stinging with pressure. I don't know why, but I felt like tears were about to burst out. I wanted to tell Max, but I couldn't. I wanted to say that I'd flicked the switch because I had to. And that I was tired today because I'd spent hours shaking and crying and silently screaming out in the darkness. And that I'd left because Raya would never like me, and

I didn't know how to fix that. I didn't know how to fix anything.

I was walking down the hall when I saw Sara getting dropped off at the front doors.

Her mother was there, watching from an open window of her Lexus. Sara walked in, not waving, and then started for the office. I think she sat there until her TA showed up.

But this time she saw me and stopped. The sunlight lit up the door behind her like a spotlight.

"You're here," she said.

I looked behind me. "Uh . . . yeah," I said. "Am I not supposed to be?"

She shrugged. "I thought you would stay home. You looked upset. Because of Raya."

"How do you know that?"

Sara smiled. "I have eyes, you know."

"Oh," I said. "Right. I guess it was obvious, then."

"Sort of. But I also watch you."

I froze. That wasn't the kind of thing you said to someone. And it wasn't the kind of thing that you responded to either. I met her piercing green eyes and then looked away. "You . . . what?"

She didn't look away. "I watch you sometimes. You're very interesting, you know."

I could feel tingles running up and down my arms, like someone was letting their fingertips just glide along, barely touching the hairs. It caused my whole back to straighten by itself. And then I thought of something else.

"Did you leave that note in my bag?"

"Took you long enough," she said.

I frowned. "So . . . you're a Star Child?"

She smiled and lifted her wrist. For the first time I focused on her bracelet; the charms were little stars. There were a few different kinds—seven of them altogether. "Clearly," she said. "Just like you."

"What?"

She shook her head. "You don't even know what you are, do you?"

"Apparently not."

"Give it time." She glanced at the office. "Do you agree or not?"

I rubbed my forehead. It was like running a marathon, talking to her. "Agree to what?"

She sighed. "I was hoping for smarter. Maybe you're more of a thinker than a talker. Tough to say. You obviously think a lot, but what about, I have no idea. Agree to help me, of course."

I hesitated, unsure of what to say. "Umm . . . sure."

Sara grinned. "Excellent. Meet me after school. Don't

even say you have football. We both know you don't play."

She started for the office, and I finally snapped out of it.

"What am I helping you with?"

She stopped and looked at me, stone-faced.

"We're going to find my father."

CHAPTER 9

I was writing in class an hour later, trying not to think about my discussion with Sara Malvern.

Daniel hurried inside, closing the door behind him. He stood there with his back to the door, trying to make sense of what he had seen. The shape. It had almost been human. Almost.

It had all started with the switch. His father had told him a thousand times to stay out of the attic, but he hadn't been able to resist. Yesterday he had finally snuck up there, slipping through the trapdoor in his parents' closet and picking his way through the stacks of equipment. There, standing alone in the middle of the room, was a computer connected to several banks of servers. It was silent—covered in dust and left alone in the darkness. But what did it do?

He saw the switch soon after. It was on the side of a boxy

control panel next to the computer, wired into the whole system. Instantly he knew he shouldn't touch it.

I sat back for a second, staring at my notebook. When I wrote, the story kind of just happened. I didn't outline the plot or think ahead or anything. It was like reading a book specially written for me. And now book Daniel had found himself in a situation I knew all too well. Should he flick the switch? He didn't have to, of course. He didn't have Zaps and he wasn't crazy and he could do what he wanted. But story Daniel was brave and smart and adventurous. He wasn't afraid of anything. And I think he would *want* to flick the switch.

His curiosity was overwhelming. He had to find out what the computer did.

He tentatively reached out, then flicked the switch. The computer screen turned on, and red and green lights lit up the servers. A message popped up on the screen:

INITIATE SPATIAL SHIFT? Y / N

Daniel stared at the screen, green letters against the black. His hand moved without him. His finger found the *Y*. He wanted to know what the computer would do now. How dangerous could a computer in his attic really be? He pressed the key.

INITIALIZING.

And that was it. He stood there for a few minutes, waiting for something to happen. But the computer remained silent, and Daniel finally just gave up. He snuck back out of the attic, disappointed. It was an old computer, and nothing more.

Or so he'd thought. As he stood there with his back pressed to the front door now, he realized he hadn't switched it back.

Daniel raced upstairs, pulled the trapdoor down, and scrambled up the ladder. He raced over to the computer. The screen said:

PROCESS COMPLETE.

Daniel sat down and pressed *N*. Nothing. He pressed escape. Another message popped up.

PROCESS CANNOT BE REVERSED FROM THIS STATION.

"What process?" he whispered. He scrambled through the papers on the desk. In desperation he flicked off the switch. The screen turned off. But it was too late.

A paper slipped out and fell onto the floor. It read:

Station #9
Please oversee SAT for 03/05/14–03/05/15. Contact

HQ if you have any issues.

Regards,

Charles Oliver

214-054-2012

Daniel put down the paper. He needed to make a call.

I closed my notebook, hoping no one had noticed. I didn't write often at school, but sometimes when I was bored, I continued writing in a notebook that I kept hidden. It probably wouldn't have helped anyone to read it anyway—my handwriting looked like Egyptian hieroglyphics.

It was English class, so I felt like I was kind of participating. We were talking about *Lord of the Flies*, which I'd read before.

As soon as I stopped writing, I found myself thinking about Sara again. I still wasn't sure if I was going to meet her. I mean, I really did have football practice, and my dad always said it was bad to skip things, even if no one would notice.

But she had asked me to help find her dad. How could I just ignore that?

"You all right?" Max whispered.

"Yeah," I said. "Just thinking."

"About play-offs? Two weeks, man."

I snorted. "Yeah. Exactly."

He nodded. "Me too. Portsmith is good. The best we've played this season. It's going to be close."

"We really need to work on your conception of sarcasm."

He smiled and turned back to the front. "Raya feels bad, you know."

I straightened. "What do you mean?"

"She didn't say it, but I can tell. She was looking at you when you went in this morning."

I glanced at her, taking notes as Mr. Keats talked.

"Why would she feel bad?"

"Probably because she knows you like her."

I looked at him, scandalized. "You didn't."

"Didn't have to. You light up like a firework when she looks at you."

"Great," I muttered. "As if I wasn't embarrassed enough."

"I have something that will make you feel better."

"What?"

Max grinned. "Taj told me he tried to kiss her good night."

"How does that make me feel better?"

He shrugged. "She said no and gave him a hug."

The smile blossomed before I could stop it.

Max laughed. "Feel better?"

"A little."

. . .

I found Sara waiting inside by the front doors, alone. After taking a quick look in either direction, I hurried over to meet her. She looked strangely solemn, staring out at the parking lot and twirling her dark hair around a finger.

"Hey," I said.

She jumped. "Hey," she replied. "I didn't think you'd come."

"Then why did you wait?"

"It's called faith," she said. "It doesn't matter what you think. Only what you do."

I paused. "Where's your TA? And mom?"

"I told Miss Lecky my mom was picking me up as usual, and I told my mom that I was staying after school for some extra work with my TA," she said. "Now, we need a headquarters."

I wrung my hands together. "Don't you, like . . . not talk?"

She smiled. She had a warm smile, but it didn't reach her eyes.

"Not to normal people. Thankfully, you aren't normal."

"Thanks . . . ," I said. "Uh . . . headquarters. We could use my house, I guess."

"Good. You can tell your mother I'm your girlfriend. I would prefer that this investigation remain a secret."

"Why?"

"Because my mother and her boyfriend have asked

that I not pursue the investigation. Because my father left a note saying not to follow him. And because I think he was murdered by my mother's boyfriend."

My eyes widened. "Murdered?"

"But of course I hope I am wrong," she said. "Shall we?"

"Okay," I said. "Follow me."

"I know where you live," she said.

I rubbed my forehead again. "Naturally. I guess I'll follow you, then."

She looked at me seriously. "Teamwork, Daniel. We will walk beside each other."

With that, she turned and walked outside, and I hurried to catch up.

Sara walked with purpose. She was an entirely different girl all of a sudden: focused and sharp. I had to half-walk, half-jog to keep up as we marched down the windswept October streets toward my house.

"You must have questions," she said.

"I don't even know where to start."

She turned and smiled. "From the beginning."

"Okay," I said slowly. "Why do you think I'm a Star Child?"

She laughed, loudly enough that I jumped. It was like an explosion of pent-up energy.

"I suppose that is a good place to start," she said. "Are you different, Daniel Leigh?"

I thought about that for a moment. Of course I was different; most kids weren't trying to keep themselves alive by flicking light switches and avoiding numbers. But I didn't want to get into that.

"I mean . . . I think I'm pretty normal."

She smiled again, almost patronizing. "Right. You're very smart as well, correct?"

"I guess . . ."

"You were in the Gifted Program," she said. "I would guess you have never had a grade below an A, have you?"

"In math."

She nodded. "You're a wordsmith. A poet. A lost soul. You write when no one is looking, and you pretend to fit in with the other kids, but you don't. You're also a toucher. Your mind is different."

I was trying to keep up, but it was nearly impossible. "What about you?"

She shrugged. "I have a photographic memory. Ask me a number on the periodic table."

"Twenty-nine."

"Cu. Copper. A transition metal and bordered by nickel and zinc. I can recite pi to a hundred numbers. I know that the first day I ever saw you, you were walking down the hallway when you were seven years old. You were wearing track pants and a shirt with the *Star Wars* logo on it. You had a bit of a mullet, and a lot of freckles.

I remember your eyes. . . . They were very blue. I looked at you, but you didn't notice. I thought you seemed familiar, but I know now that it's because you're a Star Child like me."

I just walked along beside her as she spoke, feeling the tingles running along my body like those soft fingertips. She had a way of speaking through me. I felt it in the nape of my neck and into my toes.

"Is there anything else that makes you a Star Child?"

She turned back to the street. "I won't get into the full details. Essentially there is a special strain of DNA passed down from ancient history. Every once in a while it results in a Star Child—a person of special intelligence and a pure heart. They can also be a bit . . . eccentric. Like me."

I hesitated. "What is . . . I mean . . . is there something wrong with you? Medically?" I flushed. "I didn't mean it like that. Just, the TA and the not talking, and you seem normal now—"

"It's okay," she said. "I have general anxiety disorder, bipolar disorder, mild schizophrenia, and depression." She shrugged. "That's what they've diagnosed, anyway."

Sara stopped and looked at me.

"So I am certifiably nuts, and I take five pills a night. But I seem normal now because I am. For what we are."

We turned onto my street, and I led her to my house, thinking that I was going to have to introduce her to my mom. This was not going to be good.

"Why do they call them Star Children?" I asked.

"Because that DNA is alien," she said. "You're not totally human, Daniel Leigh."

I looked at her, frowning, and then opened my door. My mom came around the corner and stopped.

"Oh," she said. "Hello."

"Hey," I replied. "Umm . . . this is my . . ."

Sara looked at me pointedly.

"Friend from school," I said. "We are working on a project together."

Sara narrowed her eyes, but then smiled at my mom and nodded. Obviously she wasn't speaking again. My mom looked dubious, but she gestured for us to come in.

"Nice to meet you," she said. "Can I get you guys anything?"

"No," I replied. "We'll just be upstairs."

My mom raised her eyebrows, and I sighed. She always fought with Steve about keeping his bedroom door open when his girlfriend came over. "I'll keep the door open."

We hurried upstairs, and Sara giggled quietly behind me. "Did she think we were going to make out or something?"

"I don't know," I said. "I guess."

"You wish."

Frowning, I led her into my bedroom and gestured for her to sit down at the desk. She walked right by and plunked down on my bed. Then she patted the spot next to her.

"Chop, chop," she ordered. "I have to be home by five." I gingerly sat down next to her, and she opened her bag. "Now, let me catch you up on a few things." She took out a photo of a heavyset man with short black hair. He had a warm smile. I recognized the eyes, though—green and strangely misty.

"This is my father," she said. "Thomas Malvern. Municipal waste specialist."

"He was a garbageman?" I asked.

She glared at me. "Municipal waste specialist. Now, he disappeared thirteen months ago." Sara withdrew a letter written in black pen. "He left this in my bedroom."

I took the note.

Dear Sara,

I am so sorry to leave without saying good-bye. It was too painful to tell you in person. . . . I hope you'll forgive me. I simply had to leave; things are not great with your mother, and it's time to go. I don't know where I am going, and I don't know if you'll be able to contact me there. I will try to write. I was never the best father, but I tried. You were the most important thing in the world to me, and I love you very much. Don't look for me, darling Sara. Take care of your mother.

Love,

Dad

I looked at Sara. "I'm sorry."

She took the letter and laid it out on the bed. "No time for tears."

"This seems kind of . . . obvious," I said. "He left."

She wagged a finger. "But here's the problem. My dad didn't write much. No letters or journals or even notes. But he did write a check once that was never mailed." She held up the check. It was written to the electric company.

"So?" I asked.

"The writing, Daniel."

I looked it over. It was similar to the note, but there were definitely differences. The letters didn't loop the same, and the writing was smaller in the note. "Maybe he was in a rush?"

"No," she said quietly. "I don't think he wrote it. I think my mother's boyfriend did."

I frowned. "Do you have a sample of his writing?"

Sara shook her head, and then patted my leg. "No," she said. "And that's where you come in."

"What's that?"

She smiled. "You're going to go to his house tomorrow and tell him the local paper is having a contest. He just has to write his name and address on a piece of paper, and we'll have our proof."

"But—"

She took out a sheet of paper that clearly she'd printed at school. It said:

Erie Hills Express Contest
Win two tickets to Florida! All-inclusive five-night stay
at the fantastic Coco Beach Tropicana. Please write your
name and address below, and you will be notified of the
results next week!

There was even the newspaper logo on there. It was pretty official-looking.

"Right," I muttered.

Sara took my hand and looked at me. "Will you help me, Daniel?"

Her skin was sending jolts up my arm. No girl had ever held my hand before.

"Sure," I said. "Why not?"

"Thank you. Are you going trick-or-treating or anything?"

"No."

"Good. Now, I was thinking we could analyze some news stories of disappearances—"

My cell phone rang, and I pulled it out of my pocket. It was Max.

"Hello?" I said.

"Where are you?" he exclaimed. "Coach Clemons is furious. You better be here tomorrow—"

"Why does Coach even care?" I said. "I don't play."

"You do now," he said. "Kevin hurt his knee at practice. You're playing the next game."

I felt my stomach drop into my shoes. "What?"

"You're playing," Max said. "Coach is having a special kicking practice tomorrow. Get ready, buddy. This is the moment you were waiting for." He paused. "Don't screw it up."

He hung up, and Sara looked at me and smiled.

"You're going to have a busy week," she said.

CHAPTER 10

"So," my mom said at dinner, watching me with a grin, "who is this school friend of yours?"

I looked up from my spaghetti. "Sara."

Emma was watching me with definite interest, and even Steve had glanced over.

"And how did you meet her?"

I frowned. "At school."

"Do you have a girlfriend?" Emma asked, leaning forward.

"No."

I returned to my spaghetti, hoping to eat and get out of there as soon as possible. My mom would ask me questions for the rest of the night if she had the chance. She was a notorious quizmaster.

"I thought you were after a girl named Raya?" Steve asked.

I felt my cheeks burning. "I'm not after anyone."

"Shocker," Steve said.

"She was cute," my mom chimed in. "Quiet. Is she shy?"

"Yeah," I said. "Very shy."

Sara had left soon after the phone call, probably sensing that I was distracted. I wasn't sure if I was more terrified of investigating a potential murder or having to play football. The combination was not enticing.

"Go to his house tomorrow after football," she'd said. "He lives at 17 Selkirk Lane. His name is John. Meet me at five thirty outside my house with a report. I live at 52 Janewood Drive."

"But—"

"I wrote down all the information for you. It's on the bed." She'd looked at me. "We're going to get John for what he did. And then we can worry about what's next for us. We have a lot to do."

She had walked downstairs and left without another word, and I'd been left wondering what had happened.

"She looked familiar," Emma said. "What did you say her name was again—"

"I have to play next game," I cut in. It was the only way to change the subject.

Steve put down his fork. "What?"

"I'm playing," I muttered. "Kevin got hurt. I'm the starting kicker."

Steve looked like he might be sick. He had played for the Erie Hills Elephants and loved the team. "Don't they have another backup?" he asked.

"Thanks."

Even my mom looked concerned. "Isn't it the play-offs?"

"Yeah."

Steve shook his head. "It pains me to say this, but maybe we should do some extra practicing. I can hold if you want to take a few kicks this week."

I was impressed that Steve actually was willing to hang out with me, even if it was probably more for his love of football than of me. But the thought of extra football was enough to make my stomach turn.

"Thanks," I said. "But we're practicing a lot. It'll be fine."

My mom forced a smile. "Your dad will be excited."

I sighed. "Yeah."

Just after nine o'clock my dad came into my room and grinned. "I heard the news."

I looked over from my computer, blocking the screen. "Yep."

"You'll do well," he said, grinning under his mustache.

"You have to stay calm." He patted the door and then started down the hall, obviously pleased. "Should be a good game!"

I turned back to my computer. He was going to be very disappointed.

Daniel picked up the phone, but the number rang through to voice mail.

"You have reached Charles Oliver. Leave a message."

He stood there for a moment, considering what to do next. He needed to find Charles Oliver's house. Maybe there was another station. Maybe there was still a way to save humanity.

He Googled Charles Oliver, but the name was too common to yield anything helpful. Then he tried Googling the phone number.

It was from New York City. A ten-hour drive, easy. Daniel punched "Charles Oliver" into New York City 411 and got eleven listings for "C. Oliver." It was a place to start. Looking to where the sunlight was sneaking in around the curtains, he recalled the shape he had seen between the two houses. Tall and as black as night. As fast as a shadow. And strangely, eerily human.

If Daniel was going to get to New York, he needed to drive.

He packed a survival kit: his laptop, charger, water bottles, granola bars, and a picture of his family in case he got lonely. He was just zipping the kit up when a familiar noise split through the house and almost caused him to topple backward.

Someone was knocking on the front door.

I finished the page and leaned back. I already knew who it was going to be.

The looks started the moment I got to school. Taj and the others watched me as I approached the group where they were hanging out by the basketball court, as if hoping that I had somehow become more athletic overnight. I know you're probably thinking that the kicker doesn't have to be that athletic, but you're wrong; the kicker is extremely important. In fact my dad often pointed out that the kicker is almost always the leading scorer of the team, and that when the game comes down to the last few seconds, it's the kicker that everyone relies on. They are the true pressure players. All this wasn't helping me at all, of course, and I felt like I was going to throw up.

"Morning," Max said, clapping me on the arm. "Ready for practice tonight? The whole line is going to be there, and the long snapper. I asked to hold for you. What do you think?"

"Yeah, sure," I murmured. "Couldn't you just kick?"

Max laughed. "You'll be fine. This will be good for you. But practice hard. This game is big, man."

"Thanks, pal."

Taj and the others came over and looked at me skeptically.

"Where were you yesterday?" Taj asked.

"Uh . . . I had an appointment. Doctor."

"Well, get out there tonight. We don't need any botched kicks."

Raya looked at me. "Leave the kid alone. He'll be fine."

I sort of resented the term "kid," but at least she was defending me. The guys started talking among themselves, and Raya stepped in front of them.

"How freaked out are you right now?"

"Highly."

She laughed. "I figured. Listen, you'll be fine. I saw you when I was riding home yesterday."

I looked at her. "And?"

"You were walking with Sara."

I stood there for a moment, unsure how to respond. "Yeah."

"She talks to you." It wasn't a question. "She doesn't talk to anyone."

I shrugged. "She talks to me."

Raya just shook her head, smiling. "There's a lot more to you than meets the eye, Daniel Leigh."

"You don't know the half of it."

She laughed and joined her friends, and I was left thinking that everything had seemed a lot more straightforward yesterday.

· · ·

"How?" Coach Clemons asked, incredulous. "We're fifteen yards away."

I had missed my second consecutive kick. I was supposed to be working my way backward, starting at the ten and going to the thirty-five. I hadn't managed to get past fifteen yet, though, which was a definite problem. That was supposed to be automatic range.

It wasn't that I couldn't kick. In the field with Steve I used to be able to kick it thirty, no problem. We used to play a lot when we were younger and he wasn't too cool for me yet. But when there were people watching and shouting and the other team attacking, it just didn't work out right. I usually shanked it to the right, sometimes bad enough that it didn't make it to the end zone.

"I would guess a general lack of confidence and skill," I said resignedly.

He threw his hat onto the ground and walked away. "Water break."

"Try again," Max said. He ran to grab a ball and hunched down. Everyone else was already walking toward the sidelines, muttering something about the kicker. He turned the laces out. "Now."

I sighed, and then jogged forward and easily kicked the ball through the posts. He clapped his hands together and stood up, grinning.

"See? Easy."

"I can do it when no one is watching," I said. "It's the nerves. And Coach Clemons."

"You have to ignore them all. Just focus on the ball and the posts."

"Easier said than done," I said, watching as Coach Clemons stormed across the field toward me. He had this flushed, sweating face that barely held on to his glasses.

Max grabbed a ball. "Come on. One more try."

"But—"

"Just ignore him. Relax. Just worry about kicking the ball. There is nothing else out there."

I shook my hands at my side nervously, trying to focus. I knew the routine: one right step, one left, and then kick, letting your cleat follow through toward the posts. I had done it a hundred times practicing with Steve when we were younger. Suddenly I felt like I could do it. Max was right. I didn't need to worry about the distractions.

Clenching my fists, I took a right step, then a left, and then pulled my leg back—

"Leigh!" Coach Clemons yelled. "I've had a thought."

I tried to look back and kick at the same time. I missed the ball and felt my leg swing upward, pulling me with it. I realized in horror that I was no longer standing, and then I crashed hard onto my back beside Max. I felt my brain smack the ground for some more lifelong brain trauma.

Coach Clemons appeared over me, looking exasperated. "Never mind," he said sadly. "It's hopeless."

My day wasn't getting any better. After changing and hurrying away before Coach could give me any more advice, I remembered that I had another problem that night. I was starting a murder investigation.

Why had I agreed to help Sara? Confrontation and sleuthing made my stomach turn. I was clearly more of a thinker than a doer.

But I had promised Sara I would help, so I didn't have a lot of choice.

I had looked up the address the night before, and the house was a bit south, toward the seedier area of town. It was about a twenty-minute walk, and I saw that the place was a small brown bungalow with untidy flowerbeds and an overgrown lawn. A large black truck sat in the driveway, covered with dirt and dents. I checked the house windows—they were dark.

I stood there for a few minutes, moving from one foot to the other. Maybe I could just tell Sara he wasn't home? Maybe I could say I had changed my mind? I pictured her—judging me, calling me a coward. She would know I had bailed out. She seemed to know everything about me.

As I was fidgeting, I stepped on the sidewalk crack.

Immediately my stomach tightened and my body started to tingle and I stepped on it again to get rid of the feeling. It didn't work. I stepped again, but the feeling remained. I knew I was in trouble now. I had to fix this or I would need to come back, and I did not want to come back here. But I was at four times stepping on the crack, which was unacceptable. I went to five steps, and then soon I was at twenty. A woman walked by with her dog, and I stopped and pretended to be reading a note until she was gone. Then I continued. I was at 121 before I was okay to move on.

I checked my phone. I'd been stepping on the crack for seventeen minutes.

A bit of annoyance flared up in me, and I decided to get this over with. I wanted to go home.

Trying to ignore the burgeoning panic flooding through me, I walked up to the door, taking out a pen and the fake contest note. With my hands trembling, I hit the doorbell and waited.

A minute passed with me still fidgeting, and I turned to go, relieved. Then the door swung open behind me, and a gruff voice asked, "Yeah?"

I froze and turned back. I try to avoid stereotypes, but I could see why Sara thought he was a murderer. He was tall and broad with faded tattoos on his muscular exposed arms, of everything from Popeye to the face of a woman.

He had a grizzled half beard stretching from his cheeks to his neck, and deep-set gray eyes that were looking at me like I was trying to sell him a vacuum or something.

"Umm, hi," I said meekly. My brain wasn't working again. Why did it insist on doing this? I tried to regain my composure. "I'm here with the *Erie Hills Express*."

John raised a bushy black eyebrow. "You're not the paperboy."

Good point. I tried to think quickly. "No," I said. "I'm going around for a big contest we're having right now. Any subscribers just fill out their name and address, and they are entered to win a free trip to Florida in the Coco Beach Hotel. It's a . . . community involvement initiative."

Nice ad-lib. If only my hands weren't shaking so hard that the paper was about to fall out. John looked at me, obviously unconvinced, but then took the paper and the pen.

"Five days?" he muttered. "Not bad. Just for two?"

"Uh, yeah," I said, sneaking a look behind him. The house was dark and sparsely decorated. I think there was a poster of a woman in a bathing suit on the wall.

He finished writing and then looked at me. There was a puckered scar running along his chin.

"You're not going to send me flyers and crap, are you?" he asked.

"No," I murmured.

"Good." He handed me the paper and pen. "Have a good one."

And then, just like that, he closed the door and left me on the porch. I scurried off his property and down the street like I had just stolen his TV. When I was around the corner, I took a look at the paper.

I didn't have a photographic memory like Sara, but I didn't need it.

The handwriting was the exact same as in the note.

CHAPTER 11

Sara was waiting for me at her street corner, wrapped in a light windbreaker and shivering. Her hair was swept across her face as she stared at the passing cars.

When she saw me, her eyes became hard. I wondered again about Sara Malvern. She completely transformed with me; this Sara was intent and fiery and completely lucid, like an army commander or something. While she waited for me, she clasped her hands behind her back, and I half-expected a lecture about punctuality.

"Well?" she asked.

I handed her the note. She stared at it, and her face darkened. We stood there in silence, and her whole arm started shaking. Her eyes started to water.

"Are you okay?"

She didn't look at me. "The note was all I had of him,"

she whispered. "I told my mom the handwriting was off, but she said he must have been rushed. She said he was in a bad place when he left. The handwriting was similar to his, of course; John must have had a sample. But this is the same. They lied to me. He killed my dad."

"Whoa," I said. "This doesn't prove that by a long shot. Maybe your dad left and they just wanted you to know it was okay—"

"My dad wouldn't leave," she said sharply. "Ever. Do you understand?"

I was taken aback. "Yeah. Of course. So, what do we do now?"

"We learn more about John Flannerty," she said. "Are you free tomorrow?"

I opened my mouth.

"After your stupid practice," she said, rolling her eyes.

"Uh . . . sure," I said.

"Good. We'll meet at my house. Bring your laptop. I better get back."

"Can I ask you something?"

She looked at me. "Sure."

"Do . . . Did . . . you talk to your parents?" I asked curiously.

Her dark eyes flashed again. "That's none of your business."

The harshness in her voice caused me to flinch. She

moved from thoughtful to angry very quickly.

"Sorry," I said. "I shouldn't have pried. I'm just . . . frazzled."

Instantly her thin white lips pulled into a smile. "I like that you use words like 'frazzled.' You're very smart, Daniel Leigh. I guess that's why you were in the Gifted Program."

"It wasn't anything special," I said awkwardly.

"I know," she replied. "I was in it too."

"You were?"

"Yes. But I was labeled 'socially limited,' and the counselors encouraged my parents to put me back into regular classes." She smirked. "That really worked out for me, as you can tell."

She was very open about her condition. If "condition" was the right word. I always found "condition" to be a bit of a strange way to describe a mental illness, since people also used the word to describe their physical health. So did she have a sickness, or did she just not take very good care of her mind, like exercising or something? I think I was spacing again, because Sara was staring at me.

"What?" I said.

"Where do you go?" she asked quietly.

"Nowhere," I said.

"Liar." She smiled. "Don't worry. . . . I think we'll have some time to get to know each other. I bet we have a lot in common. See you."

I hurried home, hoping that we didn't have as much in common as she thought.

I wanted to write, but I was too preoccupied with football and John Flannerty and the fact that I was no closer to making Raya like me. I figured Steve could help me with two of those problems. When he got home from football practice, I knocked on his door, and he sighed when I walked in.

"Now what?"

"I need more advice."

He turned back to his computer. He was messaging his girlfriend, Rachel. She was a cheerleader who was kind of mean. My mom didn't like her, so Rachel didn't come around much.

"What?"

"Raya still doesn't like me. And I have to play on Saturday morning, and I stink."

I kind of watched as he typed a message to Rachel. It said, *I just think you're spending a lot of time with Adam.* I hoped they didn't start fighting. Things got bad when he was fighting with Rachel.

He glanced at me. "Have you worked out yet?"

"No."

"Have you cut that mop you call hair?"

I paused. "No."

"So you haven't taken my advice."

"I need more practical advice. Look at me—I'm not going to win her with looks."

He snorted. "True. Here's what you're going to do. Hold on." He typed: *Yeah, well, that's what he was saying in the locker room. Don't be like that now.*

Uh-oh. I had to make this quick. He turned back to me.

"You're going to make light conversation. You're going to slip in compliments. 'I like your outfit.' 'You look hot.' I don't know . . . whatever you feel comfortable with. You're going to do all that, and then you're going to win the game for your team on Saturday, and in that moment, you're going to kiss her."

I looked at him, confused. "I think you're missing the problem. I suck at football."

He shrugged. "That's how I got Rachel. Everyone likes a hero. Be one." He turned back to the computer and smacked the table. "Are you serious?" He started typing furiously. "Get out."

I was already making a break for the hallway.

I stood in front of the light switch in my bedroom, shaking. I had spent the night reading *The Hobbit,* and I had felt better. It always made me feel better. But it didn't matter. The Routine had still gotten to me.

My hand was cramped and hurting. I had been flicking for a while, and I was two hours into the Routine in general. Everyone else was in bed, except for Steve, who had left to go fight with Rachel. I was quiet and stealthy. But there were tears on my cheeks, and I was biting my lip so hard, I tasted blood. I was stuck in the usual trap. If I didn't do it right, I wasn't going to wake up again.

It's probably hard to understand. But during the Routine, my mind breaks. I fall into the Great Space, and nothing makes sense in the world except for fear and desperately trying to fix it. I flicked the switch and thought, *You did it wrong. That was one hundred and twelve, which is 1+1+2, which equals four, and four is not okay.* Then there is only dread—the kind that sits on your back and claws at your head and doesn't let you see happiness or hope or anything. So I flick the switch again. And again. And then I taste more blood and I feel tears and I am clawing at my face because I know I am insane, but I can't stop doing it because I don't want to die. I try to think of Raya and my family and anything but fear, but it is hard.

Finally I manage to flick it, turn away, and get into bed. My mind goes to Sara.

Am I a Star Child? Is that why I am suffering? I liked that thought. It was better than crazy.

I was deep in the Great Space, but I could sleep now.

I rolled over, and the pillow was immediately soaked.

• • •

On Monday I watched as Max laid up another basket at first recess, and I jogged back into position. I was supposedly playing today, but really I was just skillfully avoiding actually touching the ball. It was my best bet to keep playing.

The weekend had been pretty uneventful: Max had dragged me out twice to the football field to practice kicking, and he hadn't let me leave until I hit from the thirty-five. I tried to tell him that my nerves were the problem, but he didn't listen. He thought everything could be solved by practice. It sounded right, but it didn't seem to be working.

Other than that it had just been homework and reading with Emma. Oh, and three terrible Routines. I think the stress of investigating a possible murder and an impending football game were getting to me. I wrote five chapters of my book trying to calm down on Sunday afternoon, so that was something. Fake Daniel was already on his adventure. Real Daniel was still busy counting his steps and crying himself to sleep. Sometimes I really wish I was fake Daniel . . . I like him more.

Taj dribbled it up the court, heading right for me. I was supposed to be covering Scott Fields, who was the portly right guard on our football team. He was obviously capable of crushing me, but he was also really bad at basketball and usually missed his shots anyway. It was the perfect pairing. But obviously Taj was hoping to target the weak point of our defense today, which was me.

"Help!" Tom Dernt called, unable to get back in time to block Taj. It was up to me.

I left Scott and went for Taj, crouching low and putting my hands out like Max had taught me. Taj pulled up, clearly surprised that I had even bothered to try to stop him. He grinned and started to dribble. I was now in a one-on-one situation. The other players stood back, cheering us on.

Taj went left, and I followed, stepping in front of him. He pulled up again, dribbling in between his legs and meeting my eyes. He had this sneer that twisted half of his face, scrunching up his right eye.

"Trying to cover me, Leigh? Bad move."

"Technically it's the right move," I said. "Seeing as how the point is to stop you from scoring."

"You're not much of a smack talker, Leigh."

I reached out to steal the ball, and he stepped back, dribbling behind his back. "I just play."

That sort of seemed like smack talk. I was proud. From the corner of my eye I saw Raya and the other girls watching from their usual hangout along the wall. Raya was focused on the showdown. This was one of those moments Steve had been talking about. Be a hero. Stop Taj, and win Raya's heart.

Or something like that.

I refocused, trying to keep my eyes on Taj's chest. My dad always said to keep your eyes on the player, because the ball couldn't go very far without him. Taj finally made his move. He dribbled behind his back and went hard right, cutting for the basket. Normally I would have followed the ball and been totally deked out, but I stayed with him, and he was forced to step back and post up—turning away from the basket and backing in. I stayed with him again, reaching for the ball, and kept him at bay.

That was when he swung his elbow around and clocked me right in the chin.

I toppled backward, stunned, and he dribbled once and laid the ball up. As the ball fell through the hoop, he looked down at me and smiled. "Nice try, Leigh."

I felt my mouth. It was dripping blood. Who was I kidding? I wasn't a hero.

Max pulled me up, giving Taj a dark look. "Offensive foul," he said.

"Only the defender can call it," Taj said, looking at me. "You want to call it?"

He was looking at me with these pitying, mocking eyes that did not make my chin feel better.

"No," I muttered.

Max scowled and looked at me, eyeing the dripping blood. "You better go to the office," he said. "That looks pretty nasty."

I nodded and started inside, holding my shirt to my mouth. I was almost there when Raya caught my arm. She looked concerned.

"Are you all right?" she asked. "That was dirty."

"Fine," I said through my shirt. "Bad luck."

"Sports are bad luck for you," she said, frowning at the blood pooling on my shirt. "Come on. I'll take you to the office in case you pass out from blood loss or something."

She grabbed my free arm and pulled me inside. I grinned under my shirt.

Maybe being a hero was about more than winning the game.

Ms. Redler, the secretary, let Raya sit in the office while she put a Band-Aid over my chin. It was just a cut, and she didn't think I needed stitches. Ms. Redler was plump with a shock of red hair and the most soothing voice I had ever heard. I wasn't sure how she worked with Principal Frost every day, but she certainly had the patience.

"All better?" she asked, checking to make sure the Band-Aid was secure.

"Much," I replied. "Thanks, Ms. Redler."

She clucked. "Be careful out there! You boys and your sports. Gives me gray hairs."

She sent me on my way, and Raya smiled and stood up as I walked out.

"Look at you," she said. "Now you're battle-hardened."

I nodded. "You should see the other guy."

We headed out into the hallway. I tried not to stare. She was wearing lip gloss today, and I could actually smell that it was cappuccino flavored. It made her dark lips glisten in the ugly phosphorous hall lights, and I suddenly really wanted a cappuccino. She glanced at me, and I quickly turned straight ahead again.

"You should probably take up a new hobby," she said.

"But I'm so good at sports. It would be a shame."

She snorted. "True. What else do you like to do? Writing, I know. Maybe you can write more."

"I'm not very good."

"I doubt that. What do you usually write about?"

I shrugged, hoping to change the conversation. "Anything. I'm writing a book. It's nothing."

"A book? What's it about?"

"It's . . . about a kid who accidentally wipes out the human race. He's left alone on the planet, and he has to try to find a way to bring everyone back."

She looked at me. "So it's about loneliness."

"Yeah," I murmured. "I guess."

"I write sometimes."

I looked at her in surprise. "You do?"

"Yeah. Poetry. Stupid stuff. I could show it to you sometime, if you promise not to laugh."

"Deal." I tried to think back to what Steve had said. Compliments. "I like your outfit, by the way."

She looked down at herself—ripped jeans and an overlarge white sweater that hung down over her right shoulder. "Thanks," she said. "I didn't take you for a fashion guy."

"Because I'm wearing clothes from Walmart?"

She laughed. "Because you're a guy. I happen to think you dress nice."

"My mom does my shopping." Did I just say that?

She laughed even harder. "You're honest, I'll give you that. Well, tell her I say 'well done.'"

I was pretty sure my feet weren't even touching the floor anymore. I was stepping on cracks like it was my job. All I could focus on were brown eyes and cappuccinos and that smile that I felt in my bones. It didn't even matter where I was or where I was going. For a second she was everything around me.

Ahead, two people emerged from a classroom. Sara and Miss Lecky, walking in our direction.

As we closed in, I glanced at Sara, but she was looking pointedly ahead. Everyone was silent as we passed, and Sara didn't look at me once. I looked back, but her ponytail just bounced away down the hall. Raya watched her as well.

"Do you ever wonder what's actually wrong with her?" she asked softly.

"All the time," I murmured.

. . .

Sara knocked on my door at five thirty. I was still recovering from another ugly practice. I had missed an extra point kick during a scrimmage, and Coach Clemons had thrown his clipboard across the field and stormed off. Even Max had looked disheartened. I was seriously considering running away to Mexico before the game. In Mexico, football was actually soccer, and I figured maybe I would be better at that.

And now I had a new problem. I had kind of assumed Sara would stop by after dinner, so I was alarmed when I opened the door and saw her standing there, her arms folded across her chest.

"Ready?" she asked tersely.

"Um . . . yes," I said. "Come in. Did you . . . Where did you tell your mom you were going?"

"I don't talk to her, dingbat," she said. "I left a note in my room saying I was going to the library. I do that a lot. No one even wants you to talk there." She looked past me, frowning. "Are you about to eat?"

"Sort of."

"That could be awkward. Can you skip it and say we need to study?"

"Way ahead of you."

My mom tried to insist that we join them, but I finally managed to convince her that Sara had already eaten and that she had to be home by seven, so we needed to get started. My mom looked past me at Sara, clearly itching to question her, but she gave in. We hurried upstairs before my mom could change her mind.

Pointedly leaving the door open, I turned to see that Sara was already sitting at my desk, opening my laptop.

"Hey," I said, hurrying over to make sure my book wasn't open. Thankfully, it was minimized.

Sara looked at me, raising an eyebrow. "Touchy much? I won't read your writing. But if you let me, that would be a real sign of trust. Star Children are supposed to stick together. It's one of the tenants."

"What tenants?" I asked incredulously.

"Just some things we are supposed to live by," she said. "You can read them online. We have to stick together, we have to always pursue truth and justice, we have to trust each other and not be so paranoid when I want to read your writing. . . ."

I just stared at her.

"Fine," she muttered. "May I use the Internet?"

"Yeah," I said. "What are we going to do . . . Google search him?"

"Done that," she replied. "This time we're going to do a background check."

"Is that legal?"

She glanced at me. "With his permission."

"And we have that?"

"I have all his credit card numbers, Social Security number, and just about everything else we need to impersonate him. I checked his wallet."

I frowned as she opened up a web page. *WE DO BACKGROUND CHECKS!*

"So why do you need me?"

"Because you're going to request that it go to your email as a potential employer," she said. "My mom insists on checking my emails. And I wanted your permission. Do I have it?"

"I guess."

"Good." Her fingers flew over the keyboard in a near blur.

"Are you, like . . . a hacker?"

She laughed. "Not quite. But I probably could be if I wanted to. Password?"

I didn't say anything. She turned and looked at me expectantly, and I sighed.

"Starwarsrules, all one word"

She smiled. "Agreed." She continued typing furiously and then sat back. "Submitted. We'll find out tomorrow if John has been arrested for anything. It's a start. But we need more."

She suddenly turned and looked at me.

"You were talking with Raya today."

"Uh . . . yeah."

She was staring at me intently again. She didn't even seem to blink when she made eye contact. Her eyes were big and oval, and every time I saw them, they were greener, like a lush Amazonian canopy.

"What do you see in her?" she asked.

That caught me off guard. "I don't know. She's . . . pretty."

"Lots of girls are pretty."

"Yeah . . . I know. But she's also smart, and funny. And . . . I don't know. I just like her. Why?"

Sara shrugged. "Just wondering. You look like a lost puppy when you walk with her."

She stood up, and I shifted backward a half step. She was only about a foot from my face; I could almost smell her breath—Listerine. It smelled like the blue kind. She looked at me for a moment.

"Girls make you nervous," she said. It wasn't a question.

"No," I said quickly. She just stared at me. "Maybe a little."

"Can I try something?"

I felt budding panic in the very bottom of my stomach. "Okay."

She gently took my hand in hers, pressing her thumb to my palm. "What do you feel?"

"Um . . . you?" I said.

"Try harder," she replied sarcastically.

I thought about that as she lightly brushed her thumb along my palm.

"I feel . . . tingling . . . electric tingling in my hand and into my arm. I feel the hairs standing up on my arm, and goose bumps."

"Good." She moved her hand up and caught my arm, right where my biceps should have been. She slowly let her hand fall down my arm. "Now?"

I could almost feel the sweat forming on my forehead. I barely managed to speak. My whole body was constricted with nervous energy. "Umm . . . more tingling. Now into my neck and shoulders, and down my back. I feel . . . hot on my cheeks."

She smiled. Then she dragged her fingers along my neck and cheek.

"Stay still. I'm going to close my eyes."

"What?"

"Just stay still."

I did as I was told. My whole body felt spasmodic.

"I call this 'the Blind,'" she said, closing her eyes. "I used to do it with my dad. We would close our eyes and think about how we would describe people if we couldn't see them. If we could only use our hands."

I felt her hand moving across my face. It was soft,

barely touching sometimes and then finding my nose and cheeks and chin, and then soft again across my mouth. I felt it more than I had ever felt anything else.

"But it's a great way to heighten sensations," she said. "You have nice high cheekbones, like a royal or something. Pointed chin, larger nose, but not too big, and nice lips. Better than they look."

I wasn't sure how to take that.

"Try me."

"I don't know—"

"Do it."

I closed my eyes, reached out, and hesitantly put my fingers to her cheeks, half-expecting her to recoil. She just stood there silently. I ran them down her cheeks, which were smooth and rounded down to her chin. My whole body was screaming with nervousness, but I kept going, running them over her rounded lips and up over her thin eyebrows.

"Well," she said. "Do I feel pretty?"

I quickly pulled away. "Uh . . . yeah. You have nice eyebrows."

She opened her eyes, smirking. "Really? Eyebrows?"

"What was the point of that?"

She shrugged. "Girls make you nervous. I wanted you to think about what nervousness actually felt like. Then I wanted you to get used to it. The only way to get over nervousness is to face it. That's what my therapist always tells me, anyway." She winked and plopped down onto the bed. "Now you have touched a girl. It wasn't that scary, was it?"

"Sort of."

She laughed. "Don't be silly. Now sit down. I want to show you something."

I sat down beside her, my skin still prickling.

She withdrew a piece of paper from her backpack and laid it on the bed. It was a blueprint drawn on chart paper. The detail was impeccable. Even the objects were identified by label and size.

"What is this?"

"John's house," she said simply. "I went there once with my mom."

"You drew this from memory?"

"Yes. Now, notice where his bedroom is. I only got a peek, but there were two dressers and a nightstand. I suspect his room is where he would keep any potential weapons, letters, or nefarious secrets."

I glanced at her. "Why are you showing me this?"

She smiled, as if I had asked a stupid question. "Because we're going to break in," she said. "But don't worry. This time I'll be going with you."

CHAPTER 12

"You're joking, right?"

I waited for her to laugh. She didn't.

She frowned. "It wouldn't be a very funny joke. Though, humor isn't my strong suit. Let me guess. . . . You're afraid."

"We're investigating him for a murder," I said incredulously. "Of course I'm afraid."

She nodded, turning back to the blueprint and studying it intently.

"Fair," she replied. "But don't worry. He works until ten thirty on Tuesdays. We have tons of time. And when I said 'break in,' I meant I stole one of his keys. We're just going to pop inside."

I rubbed my forehead, trying to remember how I'd gotten myself into this situation.

"It's still breaking in."

"Of course," she said. "But sometimes the law has to be bent to be properly maintained."

"That doesn't sound right."

She looked up at me, a small crease forming between her eyes. "Are you coming or not?"

"Fine," I murmured. "What time are we going?"

"Seven," she said. "After his last break, in case he ever goes home for dinner. We'll be in and out in thirty minutes. Bring gloves, just in case. I also have baggies and swabs for blood testing."

The color drained from my cheeks. "Blood testing?"

She waved a hand in dismissal. "Unlikely. Any questions?"

I didn't even know where to start. I looked at the blueprint, shaking my head.

"Can you tell me a bit about your dad? Why would John even kill him?"

She paused, and then neatly folded up the paper and put it back into her bag.

"Fair question. My mom and dad got married only a few months before I was born. They were both good parents. My dad and I were closer, maybe because he didn't try as hard to make me normal. My mom wanted me to be better. She was the one who always took me to doctors."

I watched her absently scratch her neck as she spoke.

"They fought sometimes, but it wasn't bad. In any case, they were obviously worried about me. I'm an only child, so I got to be the favorite by default, but I think they wished they'd had another kid."

She was still moving her fingers around her neck. It was late evening now, and the sky was almost dark.

"Why do you say that?" I asked.

"It's tough having a crazy for a kid," she said, shrugging.

"You don't seem crazy," I said.

"Thanks. But I didn't talk to my parents much either, to answer your question."

She said this very matter-of-factly too, but her eyes were on the bed.

"Why?"

"I don't know. I didn't have anything to say, I guess. But my dad and I still hung out when he was around. He left a lot, though. I don't know if it was for work. I think my mom was having an affair."

I looked up at her. "How do you know that?"

"Text messages. Emails. It was obvious, but not to my dad. I didn't tell him."

I didn't know what to say. "So, what happened?"

"Things continued. He was gone a lot, but he always came home. He used to tell me he would never leave me, and that he loved me, and that he was going to take me away sometime for a trip." She spoke with no emotion, but I noticed her eyes were glassier. Her hand scratched faster. It was starting to grasp, like she was trying to catch something under her skin. "Then one day I woke up and there was a note on my desk. The note I showed you. And then he didn't answer his cell or emails, and when I asked my mom where he went, she just said he was gone. And then John started showing up at our house."

I watched as her hand grasped at her chest.

"Are you okay?"

She stood up, not meeting my eyes. "Fine," she said. She started to walk around, and her hand didn't leave her chest. "I don't feel good," she muttered, looking around. "I feel sick."

I stood up, alarmed. "Like . . . do you need to puke?"

"I don't know," she said quickly. Her eyes were glazed over, but there were tears slipping down her cheeks now. "My chest hurts. I can't breathe. I don't feel good."

She was pacing frenziedly, her hands on her chest.

"Do you want me to call your mom?" I asked.

"No," she said. "Maybe. It's okay. It's happened before."

Tears were streaming down her flushed cheeks now. She sat on the bed and then curled up into a ball, wrapping her free arm around her legs. She was shaking. Then I knew what was happening. The Collapse.

I sat down next to her. "You get them too," I said gently.

"Yes," she murmured. "I get them too."

I waited with her, resting my hand on her back. After a while she stopped shaking, and then she wiped her eyes and sat up, looking drained. She glanced at me, sheepish.

"I didn't say I'd be the best partner."

"For me, you might be."

She smiled and squeezed my hand. "I should go home. Can you print the background check tomorrow when you get it?"

"Yeah, sure."

I walked her downstairs, and she opened the door and looked back at me.

"Thank you," she whispered.

I smiled. "Of course."

She hurried out and shut the door behind her. I don't know why, but watching someone else break made me feel a lot less broken.

Daniel crept down the stairs, his hands shaking as he held the baseball bat he'd found in the corner of the attic. The steps protested quietly beneath him, grumbling and warning of his approach. He reached the front hall and paused, unsure what to do now.

There was another knock—louder this time. It echoed through the house.

Propping the bat on his shoulder, ready to swing, Daniel

tentatively reached out and pulled the door open. He almost spilled backward in surprise. Sara was standing there.

She went to his school, but he didn't know her well. She had a reputation for eccentricity that certainly matched her now—she was wearing a crimson headband and had a croquet mallet in her right hand, along with a kitchen knife tucked into her belt. She shook her head.

"I knew it would be this station," she said. "As soon as it happened. Step inside."

Daniel backed up quickly, and she hurried in and shut the door behind her, glancing outside. She was wearing a graphic T-shirt and ripped blue jeans, along with stained white sneakers.

"Have you seen them yet?" she asked.

"Yeah," he said. "What are they?"

"I call them Portal Men," she replied, locking the door and inspecting him like he was an item at the grocery store. "They came through when you adjusted the energy frequencies."

"Slow down," Daniel said. "What?"

"Where is the station?"

"The—"

"Station," she repeated. "Where?"

"Upstairs."

"Show me."

Daniel led her up to the attic, and she checked every room as they went, her hand on the croquet mallet. She moved like a stalking cat. She made him nervous. When they reached the attic, he gestured at the computer.

"Here."

She hurried over to the computer and sat down. Her fingers flew over the keyboard, and Daniel watched, amazed, as code scrolled across the screen. Finally she sat back, frowning.

"It's locked," she said. "It's as I feared. We're going to have to go see Charles."

"Charles Oliver?" Daniel guessed.

She glanced at him. "You're not as clueless as I thought. But we have twenty-four hours to get to New York and reset the frequency, so you're still an idiot. Does your dad have a gun?"

"I don't think so," he said nervously. "Do I need one?"

She stood up. "It wouldn't hurt. Portal Men aren't friendly. Trust me."

He looked at her, hesitating. "No offense, but you have a croquet mallet."

Sara laughed.

"This isn't a croquet mallet. Now pack a bag. We're leaving."

I leaned back, already feeling a little calmer. It was nice to get a break from the Zaps before the nightmare of the Routine started. I put the laptop away and decided to go to bed. I'd had enough Sara Malvern for one night. She gave a lot of orders.

. . .

We were sitting in class the next day, and Mr. Keats was busy writing notes on the board. I was trying to pay attention, but Max was busy using the distraction to walk me through about a hundred different football plays for that Saturday. The kids in class were all whispering and muttering about the game. Apparently some of the Portsmith Potters had been posting insulting messages on Facebook, and war had been declared by our team. They called us the Erie Hills Ele-fats, which wasn't exactly accurate. I think I weighed, like, 120 pounds after a big meal.

But nonetheless, it was expected that I be outraged, so I pretended to be as insulted as Max was.

"This is the fake hook-out," he said. "If you get the sign, he's going to hut straight to you. Then you'll drop back and hit me with a pass."

I looked at him, alarmed. "You know I don't throw."

"It's, like, a five-yard pass. We've been over this."

I shook my head and turned to the front of the class. My stomach hadn't stopped turning over on itself all day. I wasn't sure if I preferred the encouraging pats and cheers or the glum looks from the smarter players on the team. Either way, I had barely been able to eat my lunch, and I loved bologna.

Mr. Keats turned around. "For today's social studies question, we will be working in groups."

Everyone sat up a little straighter. They were waiting for the next line. He sighed.

"You can pick your own. Fours, please."

I don't know why I did it. Maybe I was distracted. But I looked right at Raya with this hopeful, deluded expression. She noticed me and nodded. What did that mean? What had I done? Were we partners?

"Looks like we're working with Raya," Max commented knowingly. "Come on."

Before we got there, Clara was sitting next to her, notepad open and smiling right at Max.

"Hey," she said. "Foursies?"

Max glanced at me, and I knew he was barely holding back a groan. We sat down, him across from Clara and me across from Raya, and waited as everyone else settled in. Raya smiled at me.

"You want to ride on my coattails again, I presume?" she asked.

"Naturally."

She grinned. "Who could blame you? Are you actually going to do some work, Max?"

"That depends," Max said. "Do you want an A?"

Raya laughed, and Clara laughed even louder, flicking her hair.

"You're bad," she said, and Max just turned a little pink and gave me an exasperated look.

"All right," Mr. Keats said, cutting over the noise. "The questions are on page forty-one. Try to keep the discussions to the work please." He sat down and opened his newspaper.

The four of us turned to each other. Raya opened her textbook.

"Why does the election process—"

"Is that a new shirt?" Clara asked Max, twirling her hair around her finger.

He looked down. "Yeah. Why?"

She shrugged. "I just like it. Are you ready for the game Saturday?"

Max launched into a discussion about the game, and Raya just sighed.

"Daniel? Shall we?"

I grinned and pulled up next to her to get to work.

"It looks empty," Sara said.

We were watching John's house from a hedge on the other side of the road. I looked at her, frowning. There wasn't a truck in the driveway, but beyond that it looked the way it had the last time: unkempt and eerie. The black curtains were drawn shut like the ones in the back of a hearse.

I had found the email sitting in my inbox when I'd

gotten home. *Your background check results are in!* I had been nervous to open it, and I hadn't felt any better once I had. John Flannerty had only one charge on his record, but it was for assault. When I told Sara, she just nodded, as if it confirmed her suspicions.

"You're sure he's at work?" I asked, peering at the house nervously.

"He only has the one truck. Plus he's at work. I did my research. Are you ready?"

"Not really."

"Tough." She suddenly scampered across the street, carrying a backpack she said she'd brought to collect evidence.

I sighed and took off after her.

We reached the front door. Sara looked both ways and then rang the doorbell. We waited, listening to the wind rustling the oak tree out front of his house. Nothing happened.

"Perfect," she said, slipping the key out of her pocket. "Let's go."

She eased the door open, and I followed, feeling my heart pounding. I felt terrible, like I'd just flicked my light switch nine times. We stepped inside into the darkened front hallway. It smelled like cigarettes and cologne. An old side table sat beside the door with a long-dead plant in the middle.

"Lovely," I whispered.

"I know."

I closed the door behind me, my eyes on the hall. I felt like he was going to burst out at any moment, but the house was silent.

"Follow me," she said. "We need to get to his bedroom."

Our footsteps creaked loudly on the green carpeted floorboards. In the hall there were pictures of John on a motorcycle and in his pickup truck, surrounded by other large, tattooed men with beards and sunglasses. In one John had his shirt off—there was a huge skull on his chest.

"Where did your mom meet this guy?"'

She shrugged. "She didn't tell me, since it was before my dad disappeared. Here."

She paused in front of a partially closed door and eased it open. It was pitch-black in the room. The smell of cigarettes was stronger here, and I could almost taste the acrid burning on my tongue. She flicked on a light, bathing the room in an orange tint from a dusty old ceiling light. The room was a mess.

There were clothes on the floor, and his bed was unmade, the blanket half on the floor. My mom would have fainted if she saw this place. There were even plates and glasses on his nightstands.

"Check the dressers," she said.

"Do I have to touch anything?" I asked sarcastically.

She just snorted and hurried to the closet. I went to the dresser and opened the first drawer. Socks and underwear. He wore tighty whiteys, which didn't really match my expectations. He seemed like a boxers kind of guy. *Focus.* I kept looking through the drawers, but found nothing except clothes and one drawer with scattered things like old parking tickets and bank statements, but there didn't seem to be much there. I did check his bank statements to see if maybe John was out of money and this was some money-related ploy with Sara's mom, but he seemed to be all right financially.

"Anything?" I asked Sara, who was digging through the closet, almost crazed.

"No," she said. "Just a bunch of junk and ratty T-shirts."

"What are we looking for? Like a signed letter of him admitting to the murder? I mean, most people don't just keep evidence of murders around."

"A letter would be nice," she replied. "But any clues would do."

I sighed and kept looking. I opened the bottom drawer and saw a bunch of dress shirts that looked like they had never been worn. I was closing it again when I noticed that the shirt on the right side was a little crumpled, like it had been shoved hastily into the drawer. On a whim I pulled it out. My eyes widened.

"Sara," I said quietly.

She hurried over. "Bingo." She slipped on some winter gloves and then knelt down to pick up a handgun that was tucked into the drawer. She turned it over. She scanned the dresser, and then slowly lowered the gun.

"What is it?" I asked.

She put the gun on the dresser and picked up a watch sitting beside the TV. It was an old thing—tarnished gold and with a hand that didn't even work anymore. I wouldn't have given it another look, but Sara was holding it like it was the most valuable thing in the world. She looked at me, her eyes watering.

"It was your dad's," I guessed.

She nodded, and tears started to stream down her cheeks. "He said he was going to give it to me one day." Her hands were shaking. "I knew he wouldn't take it. He was going to leave it for me. It belonged to my grandfather. And now . . . now it's here."

I didn't know what to do. I just put my hand on her shoulder. "I'm sorry."

"He killed him."

I paused. "We can't prove that with this. Lots of people have guns. And your mom could have given him the watch."

"Do you believe that?"

I hesitated. "No."

She tucked it into her pocket. "I'm taking the watch."

I could tell from her voice that she wasn't going to argue, even though I thought it was a bad idea.

"Fine," I said. "I'll put the gun back—"

I was cut off by the sound of the front door opening, and heavy footsteps on the floorboards.

CHAPTER 13

Sara and I looked at each other in panic. I shoved the gun back into the drawer and closed it, and Sara scanned the room nervously.

"The bed," she whispered, and then darted underneath the frame.

I dove in after her, pulling myself along the dusty carpet and cringing at the piles of clothing scattered underneath. There were some socks that looked like they might have been there for several years at least. It smelled like stale sweat and mildew. I tried not to vomit.

I was quickly distracted by approaching footsteps. I froze, and Sara and I looked at each other, eyes wide.

Then black boots entered the room. They were bigger than my head. Suddenly I heard a gruff voice talking. It wasn't John's.

146 / WESLEY KING

"Hey," the man said. "Where is the money again?"

Silence.

"Where in the closet? All right. Hold on."

Beside me Sara fidgeted and pulled her cell phone out. She started recording and smiled at me. We heard rummaging in the closet and then a muttered curse.

"Not there. . . . Well, I think I'd be able to see five grand."

My whole body was shaking. *What is going on? How did I get myself involved in this? What if he finds us?* I felt my stomach turning. Sara grabbed my hand.

"It's okay," she mouthed.

She held my eyes as much as my hand, and I felt the panic passing. When she stared at me, I felt it. As before, it was like she was looking into me. I had never seen anyone with eyes like that. I was again distracted by the sounds of the nightstand drawers being pulled open. The boots were a few inches away.

"Are you sure it's here?" the man asked. "I need to get over there soon."

I could hear faint talking on the other end of the line.

"There are clothes everywhere. What about under the bed? I know you didn't want Michelle to see it, right? Maybe you tossed it there."

Sara and I looked at each other, blanching. Her hand tightened on mine. It was over.

The bed skirt was just pulled up when the man paused.

"Where?" He snorted. "You left it in your jacket? Nice one. Where is it? All right."

He dropped the bed skirt and left the room. Sara was squeezing me so hard, her knuckles were white. We waited while the footsteps trailed away, and then the door shut again.

Sara released my hand and sighed, turning off her phone. "Nothing of note. At least I know that my mom isn't in cahoots."

"Michelle?" I guessed.

Sara nodded. "So John has a gun, has my dad's watch, and just gave some guy five grand."

She looked at me. "I think we can safely start assuming we're dealing with a killer."

When I got home, I went straight up to my room and sat at my computer, trying to still my hands enough to type. I wanted to write or do something, but I couldn't. I just kept remembering the moment when those hands lifted up the bed skirt and I thought I was about to die. I pushed back from the chair, feeling my throat tighten and my skin prickling. I was disappearing.

I felt the chair sink away beneath me as the Great Space swallowed me up.

I sat there, not feeling anything. I felt like I couldn't

move or breathe or do anything but survive and hope desperately that I would keep surviving. I was so zoned out, I didn't even know where I was.

When the Great Space finally receded, I was tired. So tired that I climbed into bed and pulled the covers to my chin and tried to go to sleep. But the fear set into my bones. The Zaps became constant. *If you don't do the Routine, you won't wake up.* I rolled over and shut my eyes, but my whole body started to shake. Tears started spilling down my cheeks. Why was I so broken?

The tears streamed down my face as I brushed my teeth until my gums bled and I did the steps and flicked the light switch. They flowed for the entire two hours, and when I finally climbed into bed, they continued until I fell asleep.

It was the Friday before the game. We had practice that night, of course, and I spent most of the day thinking of ways to get out of playing. Max was getting concerned.

"Have you been visualizing like I asked you?" he said at lunch.

I paused. "Maybe."

He scowled, pacing along the basketball court. "Visualization is important, Dan."

"I've been busy."

"Doing what?"

Investigating a murder, writing a book, trying not to go crazy. . . . There was a lot to cover. I just flushed and said nothing.

"That's what I thought." He shook his head. "We have to win tomorrow, Dan. Got it?"

He looked more stressed than I had ever seen him before. His face was red, his fists clenching and unclenching at his sides like he was squeezing lemons. Now that I looked at him, I saw bags under his eyes. Max wasn't sleeping either.

"Are you all right?"

"Fine," he snapped.

I raised my eyebrows, and he sighed and turned to me.

"It's just a big game. Coach Elwin is coming from Erie High, and you know I want to be a starter next year."

"Is that it?"

He hesitated. "We heard from my dad. He's coming down to watch too."

"You don't owe him anything," I said.

Max scowled. "I just don't want to lose when he's down. I want him to know . . ." He broke off.

"Want him to know what?"

Max turned and started to walk away. "That I'm fine without him."

I watched Max go, and thought about fathers. Maybe I didn't see mine too much, but he was there. Sara's and

Max's were gone, and they had both taken a bit of their children with them.

That night at practice it was confirmed—our kicker wouldn't be back in time. His knee was still too sore for him to kick. It was up to me.

"Hut!" Max shouted, and the center threw it back to him in a perfect spiral. Max caught the ball and expertly twisted it so the laces were out and it was angled at about 75 degrees. His eyes were locked on the ball, and I caught a glimpse of the opposing line rushing forward, and Coach Clemons holding his forehead in exasperation, already expecting me to miss. I felt the anxiety and panic and started moving.

One right step, one left step, and kick. I made decent impact, and the ball sailed over the line, though it fluttered a little. I watched it, and everyone else in the line turned to watch it too, hoping that for once I was going to make it. The ball kept sailing, straight and true, and then it dropped a foot short of the bar. I had missed again.

Max sighed and stood up, and I just slumped, waiting for Coach to yell at me. Instead he raced over and looked at where we were lined up. Then he turned to me, pointing at my chest.

"It was straight," he said. "That's all I ask. We're at the thirty-five, so we only kick it if we're inside the thirty. Do the same thing tomorrow, and we'll be fine. Got it?"

"I guess."

"Good! Laps!"

A chorus of groans went through the group, and then we all started for the track around the field. Max fell in line beside me and clapped me on the back, grinning.

"See? Getting better?"

I laughed. "I missed. I think everyone is just lowering their expectations."

"Either way."

As we rounded the bend, something caught my eye. There was someone leaning against a tree with their arms crossed. Sara. Max saw her too.

"Is that—"

"Yeah."

He looked at me. "Does she actually like you?"

"I don't want to talk about it."

He broke out laughing and kept running, and Sara just sat down to wait.

She was still there when I wandered over an hour later, sweating and flushed. She didn't have a book or her phone or anything. She was just picking grass and letting it float away on the cool breeze. She looked peaceful, or at least far away.

"You watched me practice?" I asked.

She smiled. "Hardly. I can only watch someone miss a field goal so many times." She climbed to her feet, brushing off the grass. "I just didn't want to be at home anymore. I can't even look at my mom."

"We decided she wasn't a criminal, didn't we?"

"It doesn't matter. She left my dad for one. She may well have had John kill my dad."

It was silent for a moment.

"So, what do we do next?" I asked.

She shook her head. "I don't know. I don't think we have enough to go to the police. As far as they are concerned, my dad isn't even dead. He's just gone. They don't have a body or anything. We need to get more information."

"So how do we do that?"

She looked at me nervously. "John is coming over for dinner on Sunday."

"So?"

"I would like you to come too."

"Sorry?"

She narrowed her eyes. "Is it that painful to have dinner with me?"

"No, I just . . . I mean, what would we tell your mom?"

She shrugged and started walking through the park. "That you're my friend. She'll be happy."

I hurried to catch up with her, trying to wrap my head around this new development.

"And what are we going to do . . . ask him?"

She laughed. "No. We're going to use our combined intellects to ask other questions that lead us to the truth. Or you are. I don't talk to them. Remember?"

"I don't know—"

"Are you in this or not?"

I stopped. "Listen . . . I feel bad about your dad. And I want to help. But I have the game, and—"

"And it's not your problem," she whispered. She had stopped too, but she had her back to me.

"No, that's not what I meant . . ."

She turned a little, so I could see her profile. Her lips were drawn tight. "You're right. I'm sorry. This is my issue." She started walking across the street toward the sprawling field on the other side. "You did a lot. Thank you, Dan."

I stood there, seeing my way out. But I couldn't. I jogged after her. "Wait."

She didn't slow down. I grabbed her arm and stopped her.

"Wait."

When she turned, her emerald eyes were full of tears. "This isn't me," she said, her voice breaking. "I shouldn't have asked you all this. I was selfish. I just . . . I don't know what to do anymore." Her arm was shaking under my fingers. "I miss him," she whispered. "I want him back. I'm sorry."

She pulled away. Her cheeks were bright. Her eyes were wide. I could see it coming again.

The Collapse.

Her fingers found her chest, and then she turned and took off sprinting into the field.

CHAPTER 14

I was so surprised, I just stood there for a moment, stunned. She was sprinting across the field, her ponytail bouncing around madly behind her.

"Sara!" I shouted, suddenly realizing she was not coming back.

I ran after her, chasing her into the field. Grasshoppers bounded out of the way around me.

"Sara! Wait!"

She was halfway across the field when I caught her arm again. She tried to yank it away, but I held on, pulling her to a stop. She turned back to me, tears spilling down her face.

We just looked at each other for a moment, and then her expression softened.

"Just let me go," she said. "It would be better. You have a chance to be normal, Dan. I don't."

I shook my head. "No. I want to help."

"You don't want—"

"I do."

She seemed to consider that. "I shouldn't have run away."

I shrugged. "No big deal."

"I get . . . angry sometimes. And then sad. And then nothing."

I nodded. "The Great Space. It's okay. I go there too."

She smiled. "Look around us. Do you ever wish you were alone on Earth?"

I looked around. It was kind of serene. Nothing but grass waving in the breeze, and houses, and clouds lazily drifting across the sky. We were just little specks in the grass.

"Sometimes," I whispered, thinking of my book.

"Me too. You can't be crazy when you're the only one."

She spun, lifting her hands and shouting. Then she burst into laughter and rolled into the grass. She came to rest lying on her back, staring up at the sky. Loose strands of hair fell about her face and framed her eyes.

"I could stay here forever," she said.

I lay down beside her, watching the clouds roll past.

"What do you see?" she asked, and I looked at her, surprised. She sounded like Emma.

I thought about that for a minute. "Freedom," I said at last.

She smiled. "Me too."

After a while she looked at me. "I'll try not to go bonkers anymore."

"That would be nice."

"Good luck at your game tomorrow. I'd come watch, but I hate football."

I laughed. "Fair enough."

We climbed to our feet and started for home, the sun just now starting to set.

"What time is dinner on Sunday?" I asked quietly.

She looked at me, surprised, and then smiled.

Game day dawned gray and gloomy. I woke up early, though really I hadn't slept any more than an hour at most. The Routine had taken me until three, and then I had lain there until five. It was seven now, and I'd woken up twice in those two hours to go to the bathroom.

Now I just lay there, staring at the opaque light filtering in around my curtain. It felt like there was a boulder sitting in my stomach. I tried to get up but couldn't. I lay down and tried again. It took ten attempts before I just barreled out of my room and went downstairs, still in my T and sleep pants.

I opened the front door and stared outside. A misty rain was falling, making everything cold and damp and slippery. Not exactly ideal kicking conditions. I closed the door and went to try to eat something. Didn't work. I just stared at a piece of toast until Emma came in. She shook her head.

"You should eat," she admonished.

"Can't."

"It's just a game," she said. "One that you don't even like, I might add."

"It's not a game," I murmured. "It's Dad and Mom watching. Steve. Raya. Max."

She frowned. "And me?"

"You don't care about football either."

"True," she agreed. "So think about me. I don't care if you kick a goal or not."

"Field goal."

"See?" she said, smiling. "Now eat your breakfast."

She calmed me enough that I could force down the toast, but soon after, my dad strolled into the kitchen, beaming.

"Big game today, Dan," he said proudly. "You all ready?"

We had to travel to Portsmith, but it was only about half an hour away. A lot of the families of our team members traveled with us, so it was like a home game no matter where we went. Which just meant more people to watch me miss field goals and lose the game.

"Yeah."

He nodded. "Good. We leave in twenty. Go get dressed."

He started whistling as he poured himself some cereal. My stomach turned again, and I went upstairs to get ready.

The game started well enough. I had to kick off first, but I was always a bit better at that, since there wasn't a target to miss. I managed to get a decent kickoff, and Max tackled their returner at the thirty, which was pretty good. Coach Clemons even patted my back on my way off the field, and my mom gave me a thumbs-up from the stands.

Despite the weather, the bleachers were packed. Raya and Clara were there, wrapped up in windbreakers and scarves and mittens to keep out the damp November cold. Steve had even come out for once, probably hoping to see me make a fool of myself, and there, sitting a few bleachers down from Max's mom, was Max's dad. I'd seen pictures, though he had a beard now, and some gray was sneaking into his black hair. He was watching Max proudly, as if he had a right to do that.

Max was playing like someone possessed. He scored a touchdown on our first possession, putting us up 6–0. I ran out for the extra kick, trying to stay calm. *Just visualize the kick.*

The hut came back, Max placed the ball, and I took my two steps and kicked. It was silent as the ball took off toward the cloudy morning sky. And then the ball went through the uprights. I had made the kick.

Max gave me a one-armed hug, grinning. "I knew you had it in you!"

As we ran off the field, Coach Clemons patted me on the shoulder again. It was like a bizarre dream.

The game continued on through the mist and damp, but no one was cold. It was getting heated. The refs had to step in twice to stop pushing matches. The two benches were shouting at each other. At one point Coach Clemons threw his hat and stormed out onto the field, gesturing wildly about a blown call.

I didn't even recognize Max. He was pacing around the sidelines, his face red, shouting orders and getting more and more crazed. At one point he grabbed my shoulders and shook me.

"We're going to do this, Danny," he said. "You got this, baby."

He stormed away, and I shook my head. He was talking like the rest of the team. I don't think he'd ever called me "Danny." It was something Taj said all the time.

I realized I was getting a little excited. I was part of the team.

There were two minutes left in the game when it happened. We were up 31–25 when they scored. The other kicker converted, and we were down by one. It was my worst nightmare. I sat on the bench and prayed that Max would score with one second left and we wouldn't need a kick. But the prayer didn't work.

The team started the drive from our forty. A few conversions. Killing time. We were stopped again on their thirty-nine with two downs. One of our running backs, Kyle, got us a few more yards, centering the call at the thirty-four. And then everyone turned to me. Coach Clemons appeared over me, looking panicked.

He tried to act calm. "Get out there, son," he said gravely. "Make me proud."

I walked through the team like I was going to my death. My arms were rigid. I heard my mom through the cheering crowd.

"Go get 'em, Dan!"

Thanks, Mom.

I jogged out to the thirty-four, and Max took me by the shoulders again. "You can do this."

I nodded, not trusting myself to speak. My breathing didn't feel right. My stomach hurt.

But I could do this. I just had to kick the ball straight.

We lined up. I took two steps back. I was shaking terribly. *Think about Emma*, I told myself. *She doesn't care. And neither does Sara.* I thought of her, lying in the grass, staring up at the clouds.

She didn't care about football.

"Hut!" Max screamed.

The ball flew back, he placed it, and I kicked.

It felt like everything stopped except the ball. I couldn't hear Max shouting or the opposing line crashing forward or even the crowd. I just watched the ball sail end over end toward the field goalposts. I'd gotten better contact this time—no fluttering. It was the best kick of my life. And then the ball hit the crossbar.

There was a clang as it rattled off and flew back toward the field. It landed right in the arms of a Portsmith Potter who had been back to field any misses. I heard the cries. The groans. It was all over.

And then the Portsmith player did something ill-advised. He spotted an opening to our end zone and took off running. For a second everyone on our team was too surprised to act, and then they started the chase. I joined in, still burning with humiliation. The player just had to go down, or the Potters could run out the clock. But he kept running. He was clear up the sidelines, and he wanted the glory.

Max wanted it more. As I chased after the guy, Max appeared out of nowhere and hit the player so hard that he flew out of bounds, the ball sailing out of his hands. It bounced once and then landed by my feet.

"Go!" Max screamed.

I had no choice. I scooped up the ball and started running. Everything was happening fast. A Portsmith Potter closed in on me, but Taj clocked him out of the way, and they both landed in a heap. I kept running. The blocks lined up down the sideline, and I ran as fast as I could. There was no thinking. I just ran until I was at the back of the end zone. Suddenly my entire team was running toward me, jumping and screaming. I just stood there, holding the ball, and then it was sent flying by the rest of the team, all of them hugging me and patting me and then even hoisting me up onto their shoulders.

I saw my mom and dad hugging in the bleachers. Coach Clemons was jumping.

Grinning, I let myself be swept away in the celebrations.

CHAPTER 15

It was the best day of my life. The team celebrated all day at Coach's house with a barbecue. Max walked around the whole afternoon beaming—even after his dad just shook his hand and got back into the car.

It was a blur of laughter and congratulations and feeling like people cared about me.

It was nice, but the only downside was the grim fact that I had to do it again next week.

I really hoped Kevin got better by then.

When we finally got home, I was exhausted and went upstairs to lie down. I flopped onto the bed and stared at the ceiling, smiling. I hadn't gotten much chance to talk to Raya after the game, but I'd seen her smiling as I'd been hoisted across the field. She had said she didn't like football, but everyone liked a hero—according to Steve anyway.

I pictured her smiling and wondered if she was possibly by any chance thinking about me.

I hoped so.

But a part of me also remembered that the person I had pictured right before taking the kick was Sara Malvern. And I thought about lying next to her in the field, eyes on the clouds. I thought about the hair that always blew across her face, reaching down past her lips. I thought of her fingers on my cheeks.

But I couldn't like Sara Malvern. She was weird and constantly reminding me that I wasn't normal either. And I wanted to be normal more than anything else in the world. I wanted to be the kid I was today.

That night I watched a college game with my dad. We didn't do that much, but he told me to come downstairs and watch and have some chips. Steve was out, and Emma wasn't interested, so it was just us.

I cheered for the same team he did—Ohio State. I figured I had to. But even though I really didn't like watching football, I was happy to be there with him.

"Some play today," he said.

"Yeah," I replied. "Lucky, I guess."

"Sure, but you still have to make your own luck. Haven't seen a finish like that in years."

I shrugged. "Me neither. I'm just happy we won."

I was a little distracted already. I ate a chip in the first quarter, and something didn't feel right. I decided it was because I'd chewed it wrong, and ate another. Three bites. And then four. I was eating them all. I was sitting there listening to my dad, but my mind was on the chips. My thoughts were racing. *If I don't fix this, my whole day is ruined. What did I do wrong? Was it the number four? Five? What do I do?*

I was sweating a little and trying to sit still, but I couldn't. I had another chip.

"How's school going?" my dad asked, his eyes on the TV.

"Good," I said. "No problem."

My hand went to the bowl.

"All As?"

"Everything but math."

He looked at me, frowning. "Again? What's going on with the math?"

"Nothing," I muttered. "Just not my best subject, I guess."

He snorted. "You got As until two years ago. Both your mom and I are good at math. How do you stink at it?"

"I don't know." Five bites. Six. Seven. My hands were shaking on the bowl. I was sweating heavily now. My skin felt flushed and burning and tingling. Why me?

I thought back to what Sara had said. That we were

Star Kids. That we were special, and we didn't quite fit into this world. That was why she was on meds. That was why I counted things.

My dad turned back to the TV. "Well, maybe we should do some work on it tomorrow. Listen, your mom and I were talking about something. Is everything else all right?"

"Like what?" I asked, still distracted by the chips and numbers.

He suddenly seemed uncomfortable. "Are you sleeping all right? It's just that I was up last night and saw your lights on. And then off."

He didn't need to finish. He'd seen the flicking. I pulled my hands away from the chips.

"Oh," I said. "Yeah, that was just weird. My light was making this buzzing noise. I flicked it a few times, and the buzzing stopped. Was just up reading. . . . Nervous, I guess, with the game."

He seemed relieved. "Okay. I told your mom it was nothing. A buzzing noise? I'll check it out."

We went back to football, and he didn't mention it again. I waited for as long as I could, and then I took another chip.

I knocked on the door, feeling like I was about to attempt another game-winning field goal. My mom had insisted that I wear a nice shirt and khakis when she'd found out

I was going to dinner at Sara's. She was convinced Sara was my girlfriend now, despite my protests. I waited for a moment, considering running away. Too late.

A large man with tattoos opened the door. John. He looked at me, obviously trying to place me.

"Is Sara here?" I asked.

He was still frowning. "Aren't you—"

I nodded. "Yeah. I did the contest for the paper. Hope you win!" I added meekly.

He snorted and stood back. "John. Sara's upstairs. You can go into the kitchen."

I slipped off my shoes and started down the hall, looking around curiously. The hardwood floors were spotless and gleaming, and the walls were decorated with pictures of Sara. There were none of her father. In fact, I spotted at least ten pictures of Sara before I made it to the kitchen, which was a little weird. Her mother was over the stove, cutting into a roast. She turned when I walked in, and smiled, her eyes scanning over me.

She dressed like my mom, and I noticed she had Sara's small nose. She seemed like a strange match for John. She also looked very happy to see me.

"Hi," she said. "Dan, right?"

"Yes," I said, shaking her hand. "Nice to meet you, Mrs. Malvern."

"And you," she said, sounding like she meant it. "Call me Michelle." She was staring at me intently. "Drink?"

"Um . . . sure."

She hurried to the fridge. "Sit down. Sara will be here in a second. Sprite?"

"Sure. Thank you."

She put the Sprite down and looked at me again, smiling as John plunked down at the other end of the table. "So you go to school with Sara."

"Yeah."

She nodded. "And you met . . . how?"

She wanted to know how I'd made friends with a girl who didn't speak. One who was medicated and who'd had a TA her entire life. My eyes flicked to John for just a second, and then I shrugged.

"Just through class and stuff."

She smiled and went back to cooking, leaving me with John. He was reading something on his phone. His dark eyes glanced up at me, and then he put the phone away, taking a sip of beer.

"So you . . . uh . . . eighth grade too?" he asked gruffly. His hair was combed back, exposing a white scar at the top of his hairline. He had grizzled cheeks again, and I saw a tattoo exposed on his neck.

"Yep," I murmured.

"Play football?"

I nodded. "Kicker."

"Cool," he said, turning to Sara's mom and obviously hoping she would sit soon. I got the impression he wasn't thrilled about a dinner with his girlfriend's strange daughter and boyfriend.

"Sara!" her mother called, putting the dinner down on the table. It looked delicious, but I wasn't hungry. Sara's mom sat down at the head of the table and gestured to the dishes. "Dig in, Daniel. Roast beef. My specialty."

I tentatively reached out and grabbed some, feeling their eyes on me. There was a piece of paper in my pocket that crinkled—Sara's script. I had a careful line of questions to follow. My stomach turned.

"Wow," John suddenly said, and I turned to the doorway.

I wanted to say "wow" too. Sara was there . . . sort of. She was wearing a blue dress with a white belt, and her hair was tied back with a white ribbon to match the belt. It looked like she might even have had makeup on. Her mom put her hands together, looking thrilled.

"It's even better than I'd hoped," she murmured. "You look beautiful. Sit down."

Sara's cheeks were just a bit red as she sat down to my right, not meeting my eyes. She really did look beautiful.

She kept her eyes on the plate as John helped himself to some roast beef.

"We were just talking to Daniel about school," Sara's mom said. "Do you have any of the same teachers?"

"No," I said. "Sara is usually . . ." I paused. "I mean, we might. She's bright, so she's probably ahead of all of us."

Sara's lips pulled into a little smile.

"Yes, she is," her mom said proudly. "She's doing college-level math. Not a big . . . communicator."

John snorted, and Sara's mom shot him a dirty look. I just returned to my dinner. Then I felt a kick.

"How did you two meet?" I asked suddenly, sneaking a look at Sara.

Her mom seemed taken aback. "Oh. Well . . . I think it was at a function somewhere."

"Bar," John said.

Sara's eyes flicked to him, and then she kicked me again. I winced.

"Cool," I murmured. "Recently?"

Her mom regarded me for a moment. Sara had her mom's piercing eyes. "A year or so ago."

"Longer than that," John said. "Two years at least."

Sara's mother shot him a look and turned back to me. "But let's not talk about us old fogies. How long have you two been . . . friends?"

I looked at Sara, but she, of course, remained silent. "Not long. Couple weeks."

"Do you talk much?" John asked, grinning at me. Sara's mom gave him another annoyed look.

"Tons," I said.

Her mom looked at me. "You . . . do?"

"Sure. We talk all the time. Right?" I asked, looking at Sara. She nodded.

"Oh," her mom said. "Good."

Another kick. It was starting to hurt.

"What do you do, John?" I asked.

I did not speak to adults like this. Or to anyone. But my shin was sore.

He leaned back, drinking his beer heavily. "Work at the car plant," he said. "Been there for years. A few odd jobs. Construction and so forth. You know how it goes."

Not really, but I nodded. "Kids?"

"No," he said. "Not a big kid person. No offense."

"None taken."

Sara's mother obviously wanted to retrieve the situation. "So, what do your parents do?"

"Dad's an engineer. My mom volunteers and stuff."

"Very nice."

Another kick. I glared at Sara, and she glared right back.

"So," I said to John. "You a hunter or anything? Saw the big truck in your driveway."

John nodded. "Yeah. Hunting, fishing."

"Cool. What do you use? Like, a rifle or a bow . . ."

"Rifle," he said. "Scope and everything. It's nice. You shoot?"

"No. I always wondered . . . can you hunt with handguns, too, or just rifles?"

He shrugged. "You could, but why would you? I just use the rifle."

"Gotcha. So you don't even have a handgun, I guess, then, right?"

He raised an eyebrow and took a bite of roast beef. "No. Just the rifle."

There was no kick. Whew. Though, of course this also meant that John was lying about the gun. Which was not a good sign, considering we'd found one in his drawer.

The rest of the dinner went by normally enough. Sara's mom asked me a few more questions, John told a story about killing a deer, and Sara sat there silently, her eyes on her plate. It was the longest hour of my life. After some coffee cake Sara grabbed my arm and led me out of the kitchen. She took me down to the basement, and we plunked down in front a big TV. She looked at me, smiling.

"You did well."

"Thanks," I muttered. "I don't think we accomplished much."

She shook her head. "Sure we did. He's lying about the gun, he works odd jobs for cash, and he met my mom even earlier than I thought. He killed him, Dan. I'm more sure about it than ever."

"Aren't you kind of hoping that you're wrong?"

She met my eyes. "Of course. But my father would never leave me, Dan. Never. If he'd left, he would have taken me with him. We were closer than anything. There's only one reason he's gone."

"So, what do we do now?"

Sara sighed and looked at the TV. "I have no idea."

CHAPTER 16

It was Wednesday before I knew it. We were practicing every day now, so I hadn't even gotten my Tuesday break. I hadn't spoken to Sara since Sunday. I was thinking about her, though. I couldn't help it.

Most of my time was spent thinking about the play-off game on Saturday, since Kevin still wasn't better and it looked like I was playing again. The guys were all still talking to me, which was nice, but I felt like I was going to throw up every time they mentioned the big game.

I don't know if it was nervousness, but the Routine was getting longer. The night before, I hadn't gone to sleep until five, and by then I'd been sobbing quietly, and had even scratched my face without thinking when I'd been trying to stop the tears. I was tired all the time.

That night after practice, Sara was waiting for me

again. I hurried over, conscious that I probably stunk like football gear. She noticed.

"You're a little ripe," she commented, smiling.

"Yeah," I muttered, taking a little step back. "Sorry."

She waved a hand in dismissal. "No problem. You look cute when you're sweaty."

"Umm . . . thanks."

"No problem. Now, I've had an idea."

She took her cell phone out of her pocket and looked at me expectantly.

"We're going to call someone. . . ."

She laughed. "Not quite. We're going to record him. I can't believe I didn't think of it earlier."

"That wouldn't be admissible in court, remember? I saw it on *Law and Order*."

She nodded. "Unless it was done by accident. I did a little research. We're going to 'drop' the phone under his couch by accident. It has two days of battery life, even when recording. Then we come back and get it."

"How do we know he's even going to say anything? He lives alone."

Sara smiled and patted my arm. "Oh, Daniel. You must know by now that I'm far more clever than that. Shall we?"

"We're going now?"

"There's no time like the present."

She grabbed my arm and pulled me along, almost

skipping. I couldn't help but smile. As we walked, I avoided the sidewalk cracks like usual, thinking that it was not a good time to break tradition right before going to a murderer's house again. A few times I paused or took extra long steps. She noticed.

"What's wrong with you?"

I looked at her, surprised. "What?"

She just held my eyes.

I hesitated. "I don't know. I . . . just do things sometimes. To stop bad things."

She watched me carefully. "Does it work?"

"I think so," I murmured.

"Have you ever told anyone?"

"No. I don't want them to think I'm crazy."

She smiled faintly. "I didn't think so."

We didn't speak again until we reached John's street. His truck was in the driveway.

"He's here," I said. "We'll have to come back."

Sara snorted. "We can't exactly accidentally drop a phone when we break in. The judge wouldn't call that accidental, would he? Of course he's here. I checked his schedule. We're going for a little visit."

"Why?"

She shrugged. "You're going to tell him that I'm sorry I have been so mean. And that I want to make my mom happy and make peace with him."

"As we investigate him for a murder."

"Precisely."

I sighed deeply. "This should be fun."

John opened the door, and his eyes immediately flicked to Sara. His Neanderthal forehead crinkled into a deep frown. He was drinking a beer, wrapped up in a hairy hand that looked like a mitt. He turned to me.

"What's up?" he asked gruffly.

I paused. "Sara wanted to come by. She wanted to say that she's sorry she has been so . . . aloof with you. She was just upset about her dad. And she wants to make her mom happy and get to know you."

John just stood there for a moment. He was wearing a sleeveless shirt, and I saw a tattoo of a woman in a red dress on his right biceps. It flexed as he took a drink and then shrugged.

"You want to come in for a second or something, then?"

I looked at Sara, and she nodded.

"Okay," John said, obviously less than thrilled. "Excuse the mess."

We stepped inside and followed him to the living room, which was still a mess of plates with half-eaten food, and empty beer bottles. He gestured to an old, moss-green couch and plopped onto a recliner.

"Don't entertain much," he said.

Sara and I sat down, a little closer together than usual, and I faked a smile.

"No problem," I replied. "So . . . umm . . . Sara isn't a big talker, as you know."

"Understatement," he said, glancing at her. She kept her eyes on the floor.

"But she told me she has always avoided you and given you dirty looks and stuff."

John snorted. "Sounds about right. It's fine. I imagine it's not easy when some dude shows up at home."

She looked up at him, and for a moment I thought she was going to speak. She didn't. One of her hands was fiddling in her pocket, though, the other on her chest. I hoped she didn't Collapse right now.

"Yeah," I said. "She just misses her dad. . . . You know how it is. Wonders why he left and all that."

John took a long drink of beer, draining the rest. He put the empty bottle on the coffee table.

"Dads leave sometimes," he said. "Mine did too. But your mom showed me the note. He obviously cared about you. It had nothing to do with you, Sara."

She didn't look at him. Her hands were shaking again. It was time to go.

"Where did he go?" she said quietly. John looked at her in surprise, and then me. He leaned forward.

"So you speak," he replied.

"Where?" she repeated.

He leaned back and shook his head. "I don't know, kid. He just left."

The room fell into silence, and John stood up. "I need a beer."

He clomped out of the room, shaking his head, and I looked at Sara. Her face was rigid. But she slowly withdrew her phone and slid it under the couch. Then she nodded, and we both stood up.

John walked back in and saw us. "Leaving?"

"Yeah," I said. "Thanks. We should go. We just wanted to . . . say all that stuff, I guess. Thanks."

We hurried to the front door, and he followed slowly. I didn't like the expression on his face. It was suspicious and cold and said that we wouldn't be welcome here again.

But then he surprised me. He looked at Sara and said, "I'm sorry about your dad."

She held his gaze for a moment, and then hurried outside into the evening. I went after her, and she was already halfway down the street when I caught up. She was hurrying along like a brooding storm.

"Are you okay?"

"How could he?" she whispered. "He looked right at me and apologized for killing my dad."

"He didn't say—"

"He didn't have to." She looked at me, her face tortured. "We're going to get him for this."

"What are you going to do now?"

She faced ahead, still stalking along so fast that I almost had to jog.

"I'm going to make some calls."

We had two days to wait, and Sara didn't update me on her activities. I wasn't sure that I wanted to know anyway. Leaving a recording cell phone and making instigating phone calls was starting to feel like a crime drama. But I had agreed to go back with her to retrieve the phone on Friday, and in the meantime I had plenty to think about.

It was last recess on Thursday afternoon when Raya wandered over. I was watching the other guys play basketball, but my stomach was hurting, so I didn't play. I think it was better when everyone expected me to fail. Now they expected me to score another touchdown on Saturday or something.

"Having fun?" Raya asked, stepping up beside me.

Her hair was down today, just reaching her shoulders and crimped a little. I felt my knees wobbling.

"Obviously," I replied. "I'm doing my favorite thing. Not playing the game."

She laughed. "I hear you're not going to be so lucky on Saturday."

"No," I said, sighing. "I think I'm stuck out there again."

I noticed for the first time that her hands were fidgeting a little in front of her.

"Listen . . . I'm having a few people over tomorrow night. Just cleared it with the parents. Nothing big, just hanging out in the basement and stuff. You want to come?"

"Sure," I said instantly.

She smiled. "Great. Tell Max too, obviously. Anyway . . . keep up the good work."

"I'll try."

As she walked away, I turned back to the game, unable to hold back a grin.

That night I was lying on the carpet next to Emma, staring up at the ceiling. An open book rested on each of our chests—*A Tale of Two Cities* for me and *The Once and Future King* for her. Our eyes were on the stucco as usual. We had already made up an elaborate story about a lost kingdom.

"A boy called me ugly today," Emma said.

I glanced at her. "What?"

"Yeah. He threw something at me and called me ugly. And then a nerd."

She was speaking very conversationally, like we were discussing the weather or something.

"Did you tell your teachers or something?"

She shrugged. "It was a crumpled-up piece of paper. No big deal."

"Oh." I turned back to the ceiling. "So what did you say?"

"Nothing." She paused. "I cried, though. In the bathroom after."

I felt a bit of anger race through me. "Who was this guy?"

She laughed. "You don't have to beat him up or anything. It was just the first time that happened."

"Been there," I muttered.

She looked at me. "Do you think I'm ugly?"

"Of course not. You may be a nerd, though."

Emma laughed. "Definitely. So how's it going with Raya?"

"She invited me over tomorrow night. For a party or something."

"That sounds fun."

"Maybe."

Emma was silent for a long time. "What about that other girl? Sara?"

"She's a friend."

"I can't believe you have two girls you talk to now."

I sighed. "Me either."

When she left for bed, I tiredly sat down in front of my computer. I felt the familiar feeling of unease or dread or whatever it was that always led to nighttime Zaps, so I opened my computer.

Daniel grabbed his bag of supplies. When he met Sara at the door, she looked at him resignedly.

"You look like you're going on a field trip," she said.

He looked her over—bandana tying back her hair, exposed arms, croquet mallet that apparently wasn't a croquet mallet slung over her shoulder like a rifle.

"Weapon?" he guessed.

"Yeah."

His father didn't have a gun, so he grabbed the baseball bat. He gripped it with two hands and nodded. Sara checked outside, and then opened the door and hurried out into the blinding daylight.

The silence was almost overwhelming. There was nothing but wind and rustling leaves and Sara's quick, quiet footsteps racing toward a green sedan parked in his driveway. Daniel checked for tall, black shapes but saw nothing. They got into the car.

"Do you even know how to drive?" he asked her as she threw it into reverse.

She looked at him. "Does it matter?"

They screamed out of the driveway and sped down the road, turning off his street and racing toward the highway. They passed empty houses and abandoned cars and bikes. It was the eeriest thing he had ever seen—complete and total isolation. Except for her.

"Beautiful, isn't it?" she asked, watching the houses speed by.

He looked at her. "That's not how I would describe it."

She looked at him and smiled. "You'll get it. You've been alone a long time. You're just finally seeing it."

"What are those creatures?"

She hesitated. "I don't know. My father was a guardian, like yours. They were part of an order called the Watchers. What they did, I'm not sure, but we had a station in the basement. I only know that they were monitoring the spatial frequency. When you changed it, you caused everyone to slip through the rift. I can only guess that you also brought something back."

Daniel rubbed his forehead, overwhelmed. "How far is New York?"

"Twelve hours," she said. "Settle in."

I saved the file and realized, belatedly, that I had finally made it past page one. It was a start anyway. I was about to close my laptop when an email popped up.

We'll get the cell phone tomorrow at 7 p.m. How late are you allowed out? We have a lot of recording to listen to.

I sat back. Sara was not going to be happy.

CHAPTER 17

Hey, Sara. Sorry I forgot to mention . . . I can still come get the phone with you, but then I will have to go. I got invited to Raya's party. But I can definitely still come with you to get it. Sorry.

I nervously waited for her reply. Hopefully, she would understand. It only took a few seconds.

K.

I was far from an expert with girls, but I assumed that this reply was a bad thing.

The next day Sara walked right past me in the hall and didn't even look at me. I tried to go after her, but then Max asked where I was going and I said nowhere and kept walking. I still didn't want him to know I was spending so much time with Sara. Especially considering what we were doing.

At recess I kept an eye on my sister, who usually read at the far corner of the yard against a chain-link fence by herself. We were playing basketball, but the school yard was pretty open, so I could see her clearly. I wanted to see if any boys went near her, but when the bell rang, no one had gone within twenty yards of her. Good. I would have had to do something, and I didn't really like confrontation. If it was a big nine-year-old, he might have beaten me up, and that would have been embarrassing.

A lot of people were talking about Raya's party at lunch-time.

"What time you going?" Max asked me.

I took a bite of bologna. "I don't know. When do people go to parties?"

"Eight or eight thirty. I have to be home by eleven on a game night."

"All right. My mom will pick you up so we can go together."

Max smiled. "How nervous are you, on a scale of one to ten?"

"I don't want to talk about it."

I had been to a few parties at Max's house before, but

that was it. And Raya had never been at any of them. Once we had all gone to the movies, but Raya had been, like, nine seats away. I snuck a glance at where she was eating with Clara and the other girls. She noticed me looking and smiled, and I quickly looked away, flushing deeply. I was so nervous about the party that I wasn't even thinking about returning to John's.

"We're just going to sit around watching movies and talking," he said. "Trust me, it's nothing exciting. Honestly, I was going to skip it because of the game, but I knew you'd want to go."

I looked at him, scandalized. "You better not skip it."

Max laughed and shook his head. "Relax. We'll go. We can just chill after practice if you want . . . leave straight from your house."

I quickly turned back to my lunch. "Na. I got a little . . . homework."

"On a Friday night?"

"Head start."

He snorted. "You're a nerd. Just pick me up at eight thirty."

"Will do."

Practice that night was even worse than usual. I missed a fifteen-yarder that sent Coach Clemons into a yelling frenzy. His clipboard didn't survive. Everyone looked pretty glum leaving the field, especially Max. We were playing the Beaverville Badgers the next day, and they were by all accounts particularly large, mean, and good. Even Max said we would need a little luck to win it, and he rarely said that about football. Taj wouldn't even look at me. I think I heard him say he was going to consider knocking out my knee so I could join Kevin on the bench. It's funny how fast glory can fade.

I met Sara at the corner of John's street; she was waiting by the stop sign with her arms folded.

"You're late."

"I had to go home and shower."

"Whatever," she said. "Let's move. I know you have a party. Let's grab the phone and get moving."

"Sorry about that—"

"It's fine. You're doing me a favor, and I appreciate it. Let's go."

I followed her to the house, thinking about the Sara in my book. Right now I could picture her with a bandana and a fake croquet mallet. The real Sara snuck up to the porch like a professional burglar—crouched over and moving lightly on the tips of her white sneakers. She rang the doorbell, and then stuck the key in and pushed the door open, letting me go inside first. It was dark.

Sara shut the door and nodded toward the living room. I led the way, my eyes on the kitchen at the end of the hallway. I had already spent way too much time in this house. We reached the living room—still covered in dirty dishes and beer bottles—and Sara scooped the phone up from under the couch.

"Still on," she marveled, showing me the screen. "Stopped recording, though. Must have run out of memory. Hopefully it lasted a day or so. Either way, pretty impressive." She stopped. "Uh-oh."

"What?"

"I have a text from my mom," she murmured. "John is coming to the house at seven thirty. She wants to know if I'll be back for dinner."

"I thought he works until ten!"

She shrugged. "He must have gotten off early. And if he comes here first to change—"

"Let's go."

She nodded and left the room. I had started after her, when something very bad happened. I got Zapped. It happened when I stepped off the rug. I felt the rush of dread and panic and realized if I didn't fix it now, I might not be able to get into the house again. I might not be able to fix it. I stopped and stepped back on quickly, trying to fix it before Sara noticed. She rounded the corner into the hall-way, and I stepped off the rug. It still wasn't right. Panic flooded through me now like a wave of tingling acid. I was in trouble. I couldn't leave it like this. I had to fix it. I stepped off again. But it wasn't right. Four, of course, was wrong. Five missed. Six was wrong. Seven was a miss.

Sara popped her head in. "What are you doing?" she hissed. "We have to go!"

"Coming!" I said tensely, starting toward her. When she disappeared, I went back.

I was in full zoned-out mode now. The Great Space was coming, and I needed to save myself quickly. I needed to get to ten. But when I was at nine, she returned.

"Dan!"

"Go ahead!" I said. "I'll catch up."

She scowled. "I have to lock it, dummy. What is it?"

I tried to readjust my feet. To fix it without her seeing. She saw it.

"Now's not the time," she said quietly.

"I just need to—"

"Daniel," she said. "We're in a murderer's house. We have to leave. It isn't important."

I don't know what happened. My vision was suddenly blurry. I felt hopeless and crazy and lost.

"It is important," I replied.

She met my eyes. She was looking through me again. I tried to let her carry me away. She walked over and took my hand, still holding my eyes.

"You are stronger than your fear," she whispered, squeezing my fingers. "You can do this."

I felt tears spill down my face, and I nodded. "Okay."

I was just following her out when headlights lit up the hallway. John was home.

CHAPTER 18

I looked at the window. "We're dead."

"The back door," she said, panicking. "Go! I'll lock the door."

We ran out of the living room, and I turned left while she sprinted to the right to lock the front door. I emerged into a filthy kitchen and spotted the patio doors. I fidgeted with the lock, my fingers shaking so hard it was tough to grab the little switch, and then I pulled the door open. Sara came flying down the hall after me, her eyes wide. She waved, mouthing "Go!" The front door lock clicked open in the background.

Sara bolted past me, and I closed the door, unable to lock it.

The backyard was fenced in, but there were tall shrubs in the back corners. I just spotted Sara diving headfirst behind one, and followed her, plunging headlong into the scratching, clawing branches. I landed with a thud in the dirt beside her. The lights in the hallway flicked on.

We crouched next to each other, watching as a silhouette passed by the patio doors. I could hear people in their backyards and a TV through an open window and a cricket in another shrub. I heard the sounds but couldn't process them. The Great Space had taken me again. I knew I had taken nine steps off that carpet, and that was not a good thing at all. I feared I wouldn't ever feel right again.

We waited until we saw the lights flick off and heard the truck pull out of the driveway again.

Sara looked at me, mostly shadow in the dark.

"Are you okay?"

"Fine," I said, but I knew my voice was distant. I knew I wasn't fine. I was as crazy as she was.

"Star Kid," she whispered. "You have to pay the price to be special." She stood up and started for the gate. "Let's go. You have a party to get to."

When I walked into the party, I was just returning to normal. It had been a strange walk home. I'd been completely spaced out and had mostly just mumbled "yeah" to Sara as she'd talked excitedly about reviewing the recording. She wanted to do it together and asked if I was free Sunday afternoon. I was, of course.

When I'm in the Great Space, it's easy to make plans. I don't think about the future or the past, so it doesn't matter. I'm just struggling to figure out whether I'm walking in a dream.

Before she left, she turned to me. "Do you ever read things online?"

"Yeah," I murmured.

"What about?"

"Movies. History. I like to read about authors. World events." I shifted uncomfortably. "Fashion."

"But nothing about . . . disorders?"

I looked at her, frowning. "No. Why?"

She smiled. "Just wondering. Have fun at your party. Splash some water on your cheeks when you get home." She put her hand on my shoulder. "You're still here, Daniel Leigh. Everything fades."

She disappeared into the streetlights, and I wandered home.

An hour later I entered a world of noise and laughter. There were about fifteen people there, all huddled together in the rec area of Raya's basement. She lived in a big, modern house at the end of a cul-de-sac. Her mom answered the door, and I saw her dad watching TV in the other room. His slender fingers were tapping on his cheek. I sensed he didn't like that there was a party in his house.

I'd had a whole plan to introduce myself to them and be charming in case my dream ever came true and I started dating Raya, but I was still kind of shaken up, so I just smiled meekly and hurried downstairs after Max.

Raya was sitting on the couch with Clara, who immediately threw herself up to hug Max. She gave me a quick one-armed hug that took me off guard, but I guess that was a party thing.

I found a spot on the couch, crammed between Tom Dernt and a girl named Laura. There were at least five different conversations and a movie all happening at the same time, so I wasn't exactly sure what to do. There were bowls of chips and sodas on the table, so I ate a chip and figured I would just do that for a while.

Then Raya appeared over me.

"You made it," she said. She had her hands out. Did she want a hug?

I shot up like a cannon and awkwardly gave her a hug, trying not to smell the coconut shampoo in her hair. When we released, she didn't step back, and we were only a foot away. She was wearing sparkly lip gloss. She smiled, and the little dimple appeared. I tried to remember how to say stuff.

"Thanks for having me," I managed, trying to look casual. "Nice house."

She smiled. "I had to save up a really long time for it.

Come over here. Jay is trying to argue that *The Terminator* is the best movie of all time. You have to help me put him in his place."

"And what movie are we arguing for?"

She looked at me like it was obvious. "*Love Actually.* Let's go."

Before I knew it, I was sitting next to Raya. Like, close. We were actually touching legs, and I was tingling so much, I forgot what normal felt like. Eventually I managed to convince Raya and Jay that they were both wrong, and everyone decided to watch *The Shining* next, which was definitely not my choice, because I hate horror movies and would probably have nightmares. But I couldn't admit that.

"Are we going to play any games tonight?" Taj asked loudly.

"Like what?" Raya said.

He shrugged. "Spin the bottle? I don't know."

"Let's play!" Clara said, giggling.

I exchanged a look with Max. He didn't look thrilled. I wasn't either. The mere thought of kissing someone sent my stomach into a backflip. What if I did it wrong? What if they all laughed at me? What if I had to kiss Raya and she said no?

There was no time to think. We were all sitting in a big circle in a matter of minutes. Clara was still giggling, Taj was talking really loudly, and I was sitting directly across from Raya Singh. Max was next to me, and he was quiet as well.

"I'm up!" Taj said, leaning forward and spinning a soda bottle. It landed on Max. "Just like I planned," he said over the laughter, winking at Max. "Ready?"

"Spin again," Max said, laughing.

He spun, and it landed on Ashley, and they exchanged a quick peck, though Taj tried to hold it a little longer. She sat down, shaking her head, and everyone broke out laughing again. I tried to laugh too, but I was feeling sick again, I was so nervous. I kept shooting little glances at Raya.

Tom Dernt and Ashley went before it was Clara's turn. She spun, and it landed on me. I don't even want to know how red I must have turned. Max looked at me, breaking out in laughter as everyone cheered and teased and Clara scowled like it was the worst thing that had ever happened to her. She crawled forward, and Max pushed me along to do the same. I thought I might puke. That would not be cool. I made it to the middle of the circle, and we pecked to more cheers. Her lips were really soft and tasted like strawberries, but I was way too freaked out to enjoy it. She retreated like I had tried to attack her or something. I slunk back to my spot, still burning with embarrassment. Max patted my back.

"Nice work."

"Thanks," I murmured.

I was still trying not to meet anyone's eyes when Raya spun the bottle. It landed on me.

I didn't even realize what was happening at first. Then I heard Taj shout "He rigged the bottle!" and I looked up to see the bottle and Raya behind it, smiling at me shyly. For a moment I only saw her.

She started toward the bottle. This time I didn't need a shove.

I made my way toward her, trying to remember where I was and what I was supposed to be doing. I just kept looking at her eyes and her smile.

We met at the bottle, paused for a moment, and then kissed.

She held it for just a second, and I wasn't about to be the one to break it off. Our lips met fully—not like the bare touch from Clara. I felt my lips push in, full force, and I didn't hear anything else. That is, until I heard a deep angry voice from the stairs.

"Raya Senya Singh!" her father snapped, looming on the stairs. "Get up here *now*."

CHAPTER 19

The party ended early. Raya came back and said everyone had to leave, looking humiliated and miserable and angry.

"My dad's a nut," she said. "Sorry. Next time Clara can host."

I was hiding in the background next to Max. When Raya had hurried up the stairs, her father had given me a look that was pretty much the scariest thing I've ever seen. I didn't think I was welcome back anytime soon. As people called their parents and we filed toward the stairs, I tried to stay close to Max and Taj so I could hide behind them. Raya was at the bottom, saying good-bye to people.

"Sorry," she said when I walked by. "Kind of awkward."

I managed a smile. "Best first kiss ever," I joked.

She laughed. "Just like I always dreamed."

And with that, I was past her, and when I got upstairs, her dad was in the living room, so I scurried to the front and put my shoes on. He glanced over, and his dark eyes flashed through his glasses.

"We can walk," Max said.

"Yeah."

We hurried outside and started down the street, shoving our hands into our pockets against the evening cold. It was November now, and the wind was biting. Scattered leaves were already blowing along the street. We kicked through them as we walked. Max glanced at me.

"Worth it?"

"Totally."

He nodded. "Figured. You went from zero to two tonight. Not bad."

"What can I say? I'm a playa."

"Never say that again."

I laughed. "Agreed."

We cut across a park to the other end of town.

"How many have you kissed?" I asked.

"Too many to count."

I stared at him, and he sighed.

"Zero."

I shook my head, watching the blanket of stars overhead. I was still thinking about the kiss.

"How is that possible? Every girl in school likes you."

He shrugged. "Just haven't gotten there. I don't know. I'm sure I will in high school."

As we crossed through the darkness, I suddenly broke out laughing.

"What?" he said.

"I kissed someone before you."

He scowled. "Luck."

"It still counts."

"Just try to refocus for the game tomorrow," he said. "It's going to be a tough one."

I sighed as we turned onto the street, lit up with the warm orange glow of the streetlights. The stars faded in the light, and we continued on toward the intersection where we would split up.

"Why did you have to ruin my night?"

Max laughed and clapped me on the shoulder. "You'll do great."

"And if I don't?"

"Then I get to kick your butt after the game."

I smiled. "Deal."

When I got home, the house was quiet and still. Emma was asleep, and Steve was still out, probably at a party somewhere. He was always at a party somewhere. I crept upstairs, my footsteps loud in the silence even as I tiptoed along, hoping to not wake my mother. Dad slept like a log, but Mom was always on the edge of alertness, waiting for Steve and me and never quite resting. I knew the feeling. Sometimes I felt like I never rested either. . . . There was always a thought or Zap or fear waiting for me.

But that night I was still glowing from the kiss with Raya. I knew there was just a hint of lip gloss still on my own lips, but I was not going to clean that off. I kept getting little hints of strawberry like she was still there. The Routine was faster that night. One hour and forty-two minutes to get to bed, and only because I got Zapped crossing the bedroom with eight steps, and I had to go back. It took thirty minutes to cross the bedroom, and by the time I lay down, my legs were sore and aching.

But even then I could taste the strawberries, and it pushed the fears away.

I slept soundly, hoping for a thunderstorm to cancel the game in the morning.

There's only so much luck to go around, I guess.

It was rainy and cold, but there was no lightning. In Erie Hills you have to have some serious lightning to call a game off, and cold weather certainly wasn't going to do it. And so we marched out onto the field in the misting, clinging haze that slunk underneath my uniform and sunk deep into my skin. I was shivering by the time I lined up for the kickoff.

The Badgers were huge. From the other side of the field, they eyed me like their namesake—all dark eyes and twitching muscles and looking at me like I was a rabbit and certainly not an elephant. Despite the weather the stands were packed again, even more than last time, with the traveling Badgers fans that made up their own troop on the far side. Parents were standing and cheering and watching.

Raya was there too. She and Clara were huddled up in rain slickers and hats, watching from the second row. I caught her eye, and she smiled and gave me a wave.

I felt my stomach weaving itself into a pretzel again. Last night felt really far away.

The whistle blew. I pulled my leg back to kick and didn't really plant the other one. I hadn't practiced much in the rain. As a result, I felt my left plant leg sliding forward inevitably as I kicked.

It was like I slipped on a banana peel. I spilled backward, barely connecting with the football and sending it dribbling down the field. I landed in the mud with a splat and a very ungraceful flapping of my arms. I sank an inch deep. I could hear the laughter in the stands.

Good start.

The rest of the game didn't go much better. The Badgers were a great team, and they had one player in particular who might as well have been playing for Penn

State. He was a big, burly kid with curly red hair poking out below his helmet, and legs like pistons. Apparently his name was Curt Stoughton, and he was being scouted out of eighth grade. As he crushed another one of our guys, I could see why.

Luckily for us, Max was also having the game of his life. He scored three touchdowns before half, including an amazing diving catch in the end zone that sent the parents into a frenzy. I heard his mom screaming out from the bleachers as he ran back to the sidelines, grinning.

And then there was me. I managed to kick off the ball successfully twice, but also managed to fall yet again on another. I only made one extra point out of three attempts, and Coach Clemons hadn't even tried me on a field goal yet, despite the team's being in range on several occasions. We punted from thirty yards at one point, which was definitely in my range. I didn't mind. I would have punted from the ten if we could.

There was a minute left in the third when my luck ran out.

We closed in to the twenty-one and then got stopped on third down after Curt burst through our offensive line and sacked our quarterback for the fifth time. He was relentless. Everyone turned to me.

Sighing, I started to trot out to the field, when Coach caught my arm.

"You can do this, Leigh," he said, his fingers tight on my elbow. "We practiced for this. Thirty to twenty-seven. Big play here. You can level us up. You all right?"

"I think so—"

"Good. Get out there."

I ran out to the lineup, and Max just nodded at me and lined up for the hold. We were just a bit to the left, and I knew I had to kick it nice and straight or it would hook left in the wind. Nice and straight.

"Hut!"

The ball flew back a bit high. Luckily Max was there, because he caught the tough snap and managed to get it down and save a disaster. But it took longer than usual. Curt crashed through our front line like a bulldozer, closing in fast. I had a second or two at most. I sped up my steps and prepared to kick, knowing I was probably too late. Curt was going to block it. I think Max realized it at the same time.

He pulled the ball away at the last second, after I had already started my kick. My leg sailed clean through where the ball had been, and I slipped backward with the momentum. Curt was diving forward, his mitt-like hands spread wide for the block. He caught my cleat instead. My right foot smashed into his hand, and I heard him shriek as my foot connected with his fingers. We both crashed to the ground beside each other as Max was tackled to our right, clinging to the ball.

I looked over and saw Curt holding his hand. One of his fingers was bent sideways.

"Uh-oh," I murmured.

He was helped off the field soon after and taken to the hospital. I heard someone say he'd broken two fingers. Without their star, the Badgers fell apart. Our offense started to pick them apart, and we won comfortably at fifty to thirty-eight. When the clock ran out, Coach Clemons came straight to me and shook my arm gleefully.

"You did it again, Danny. You're a good-luck charm. State finals next week. You're in."

With that, he went to join the celebrations, and I sank onto the bench.

Not again.

The highways were longer when they were empty. The countryside rolled past—hills and moors and little towns clumped together like mushroom caps. Daniel and Sara saw no more shapes, but there were still birds flying overhead, untroubled by the emptiness below.

Sara drove with her eyes locked on the road, fiery and intent. Daniel knew her from school, but he had never seen her like this. She was shy and distant and peculiar, sticking to herself and mostly reading in the corners. Now she was a warrior. A survivor.

"What else do you know about the stations?" I asked.

She shrugged. "Only what I managed to overhear from my

father. He would never tell me anything. But I know they are called Watchers and that the stations link together in a certain pattern. He told me that most people think you can only find space by going out. He said you could also find it by going in. I think he meant dimensions. Alternate realities."

"And so you think I opened a door."

"Exactly. The humans went in, and something else came back out."

"But why not us?" Daniel asked.

"Obviously we're special," she replied. "Different somehow. And it's our job to fix it."

She went silent for a moment.

"And I want to find my dad."

Daniel let the silence hold for a while again. "Do you think we can save them?"

"I hope so. Once we get to New York—"

She was cut off by a tree flying out onto the street. Sara slammed on the brakes, and we skidded sideways, both of us crying out as the tree raced toward us. We stopped just in time, missing it by inches. Sara and I looked at each other, eyes wide.

"How did—" I started.

I didn't finish. A shape suddenly appeared behind Sara, tall and slender and as black as night.

My fingers were flying over the keyboard when my cell phone rang. I almost fell off my chair in surprise. It was after midnight. I looked at the phone and frowned. Sara.

"Hello?" I said uncertainly.

"Are you sleeping?"

"No."

"Good. I'm outside."

I looked at my window. "What? Where?"

"Disney World," she said sarcastically. "Where do you think? I couldn't wait until tomorrow. I listened to it. You need to hear this. Can I come in?"

I paused. My mom would not be happy.

"On my way."

I eased the door open and let her in, and then we both crept down to the basement. She jumped onto the couch and laid the phone out in front of her, nodding at me to sit. I sat next to the phone, staring at it apprehensively.

"What is it?"

"Listen."

She hit play, and we sat there in silence. Then I heard shuffling and movement and a TV playing in the background. It sounded like a football game. And then a phone rang. There was a groan and heavy steps.

"Hello," a gruff voice said. John. "Fine. What's up?"

I looked at Sara, still feeling weird about invading his privacy like this. She kept her eyes on the phone.

"That's fine," John continued. "I'll be here all day Saturday. Except for dinner. I'm over at Michelle's. . . ."

Yeah, that's still going. . . . I know. There was a lot of complications. The girl is still weird."

I glanced at Sara, but she still showed no reaction.

"I don't know. Michelle told me . . . the girl's got ten different disorders. Doesn't speak. Walks around like a ghost. . . . Yeah, well, got it from her dad, I guess. . . . I know. It's been almost a year."

Sara leaned in intently, gesturing for me to do the same. John's voice was quieter.

"Yeah. Messy one, that. Wish I hadn't had to get involved, but Michelle said it was necessary. She asked me to do it. I told her to leave it alone, but she knew the girl would have questions. Close to her dad, I guess. So I did it, and it seemed like it was fine. Lately I don't know. She's acting weird again."

Sara's hands were shaking again. I stared at the phone in amazement. It was all true. John had killed him, and he didn't even seem to mind. It was like he was talking about cutting the grass or something.

"Michelle's worth it," John said. "She's a good one. Just a shame about everything else. But yeah, we can chat more Saturday. Two? . . . Sounds good. Take it easy."

The phone call ended, and Sara turned off the recording.

"It was all I got," she said quietly. "And all I needed."

"It's not proof," I murmured. "But I believe you now. So, what do we do?"

Sara met my eyes. "We figure out a way to take him down." She stood up and started for the stairs. "I should get home."

I noticed for the first time that she was wearing a backpack. I followed her upstairs and out onto the front porch. It was bitingly cold, and I shivered in my sweater and sleep pants. She turned to me.

"Two nights ago I came to talk to you late," she said.

I frowned. "You did?"

She nodded. "I couldn't sleep and I wanted to go over some clues with you."

"So why didn't you?"

Sara paused, glancing up at my bedroom. "How long does it take you to go to sleep?"

A different kind of chill suddenly ran down my back. "Why?"

"I'm sorry," she said. "I shouldn't have stayed. The curtains were mostly drawn. But not all the way. I waited for an hour and watched."

I didn't say anything. Shame and humiliation and even anger swept through me. She reached out for my hand, but I pulled it away. She continued.

"The lights flicked. Sometimes nonstop, and then they

would pause, and then go again. It was still going when I finally went home. How long does it take you to go to bed?"

My eyes were unexpectedly welling with tears. I looked away. "A while."

"What does it feel like?" she whispered.

I didn't reply for a moment. "Like I'm dying every night. Like I go mad."

"And you don't know why?"

I shook my head, and the tears started to drop. I felt my face burning with embarrassment. My knees suddenly felt weak, and I wanted to just drop. I was always hiding, and someone had still seen me.

"I don't know what's wrong with me," I managed, my voice cracking. "Maybe I'm being punished for not being a good kid all the time or something. Maybe I am not a good person or—"

She found my hand, and this time I let her. "I told you," she said. "You are extraordinary. No one said that it would be easy."

I felt my face scrunch up like a dishcloth, closing in above my nose. Tears flowed.

"You never looked it up online, did you?" she asked.

"What would I look up?"

"And you've never told a soul?"

I shook my head. "I don't want them to know."

"Of course," she said. She let go of my hand and slipped off her backpack. As I watched, she withdrew a book, seemed to think about something, and then handed it to me. "Read this," she said. "I got it from my doctor's office. If you want . . . call me tomorrow."

She hurried away, and I turned over the book, reading through blurry eyes.

OCD: How Compulsions Can Take over Our Lives.

CHAPTER 20

I spent most of the night reading. It was lucky the next day was a Sunday, because I didn't get to sleep until the sun came up. I read and reread and counted and cried silently from confusion and relief and doubt and so many emotions that by the time I slept, I felt like an empty well.

It was all there. From the beginning I knew.

OCD stands for obsessive compulsive disorder and is an anxiety disorder. Some believe it is a brain disorder, caused by the malfunction of a component of the brain called the amygdala. The disorder has two parts: obsessions and compulsions. These obsessions and compulsions take up considerable time and cause tremendous suffering for the individual. The sufferer believes that their obsessions and compulsions are central to their well-being, and sufferers can sometimes create intricate explanations to justify the continuance of their rituals. The fears could be:

- Sanitation (fear of germs, disease)
- Scrupulosity (fear of offending a higher power or acting contrary to your morals)
- Personal Health Fears (fears of dying, choking, going insane)
- Responsibility Fears (fears of harm coming to others)

These fears cause the sufferer to create rituals to relieve the uncomfortable and highly distressing anxiety that follows. When the person conducts a ritual, the anxiety lessens, and the person feels better. But as soon the anxiety returns, the sufferer must complete the ritual again or face even greater torment.

When I finished reading, I lay there and thought about it. I had OCD. It made sense. It was a disorder.

The Zaps were caused by anxiety. The things I did—the counting and the rituals—were just ways that I tried to control the anxiety. The obsessions made me want to do things, and it was called a compulsion when I actually did it. I didn't get hit with Zaps as much when I was talking to people or actually playing football, because I was too busy to notice the anxiety. At nighttime I noticed it the most, and that was when I really fell apart. The Routine was just a long ritual. Even the other parts had names. The Collapse was called a panic attack. The Great Space was called derealization. It was all there.

My mind was reeling. I wasn't alone. There were other people with this sickness.

And then I got up and started the Routine. It took me three hours.

When I woke up, I saw the book lying beside me and I swept it under the bed before anyone else saw it. I didn't know what to think. There was a small relief to know there were other people who had OCD, but now I was officially a crazy person. I was just like Sara after all. We weren't extraordinary.

We were mad.

All I ever thought about was being normal. I dreamed about it and pretended I was and that the Zaps weren't really happening. But now it was confirmed. I wasn't normal. I never had been.

I called her. I sat perched on the corner of my bed, arm wrapped around my knees. She picked up quickly, like she was waiting for the call.

"How long did you know?" I asked.

"I suspected two years ago," she said. "I saw you in class once with your textbook. Flipping a page and rereading the sentences. I looked it up later that day."

I dug my fingernails into my cheek, not thinking. "Why didn't you tell me?"

"We didn't talk then. And you read so much . . . I figured you knew."

"I didn't think . . . I didn't know it was a disorder. I thought I was the only one."

"We always do," she said. "You should be happy."

"Happy? I thought I was special. I'm just crazy."

Her voice lowered. "You have OCD, Daniel. But you're still extraordinary."

It was silent for a moment.

"Can we go for a walk today?" she asked.

"Okay."

"Meet me at your corner at one. Bye, Daniel."

She hung up, and I stayed there for a while longer, wondering if she was right.

I did a bit of writing before I went. It was the only thing I could do that made any sense. I got to control everything. It was my world and my story, and I could delete a sentence if I wanted to, and it would be gone. Maybe there was more to it too. The Daniel in my book was normal. He was saving the world. He was the Daniel I wanted to be.

Sara slammed her foot down on the gas pedal, and the car shot past the creature, barely missing its outstretched hands. She whipped the car into a turn around the fallen tree and sped back onto the highway, and Daniel turned to see the creature leap over the tree after them.

He could see it better now. It was at least seven feet tall and as thin as he was; its arms were long enough to reach its knees and ended at slender fingers, at least a foot long. Its face was long and slender as well, with big black eyes, slits for nostrils, and a small flat mouth. It was darker than anything he had ever seen, like walking oil that swallowed up the daylight.

It was also terribly fast. Even as Sara sped down the road, it lashed out, just missing the bumper. Daniel turned to Sara, wide-eyed. "That was too close."

She nodded. "Apparently they are hunting us now."

"How much further?"

She checked the clock. "Seven hours." She glanced at him. "And we're going to need gas."

I wrote two more chapters and then realized it was one o'clock. It was time to be crazy Daniel again.

We walked to the huge open field to the north of town, which ran off along into farms that stretched as far as you could see. It was flat enough that the world disappeared somewhere between the sky and the wheat fields, and it was hard to tell which was which. The vanishing point.

It's a word they use for art a lot—the place where you don't need to paint anymore because everything becomes one. We walked toward it, but of course we would never reach it. You can never vanish, but everyone else can.

We didn't say too much. We just walked in a strangely comfortable silence, small beneath the open sky. A memory came back to me of the last time I'd been in this field.

It was at school last year. My seventh-grade teacher was Mrs. Saunders, who was quite different from Mr. Keats. She liked students more than the newspaper.

I think she liked me. She told me I was equal parts smart and unusual. I know the second part sounds mean, but she meant it in a positive way. I understood what she was saying. She would assign us to write about our weekends, and one time I ended up discussing Middle Eastern politics and how colonialism was still relevant in modern-day politics. And she wrote:

You are a curious boy sometimes. But this is brilliant. I didn't even know about the secular lines derived by backward-thinking European colonists that failed to respect the nuances of indigenous culture. Your writing is meticulous and absorbing, as always.

P.S. Did you read something about this on the weekend? Not sure I see the relation. But brilliant.

Anyway, I was secretly pleased, and my cheeks were burning when she gave it back to me, and she smiled and said "good job" really loudly.

I was in the hallway putting my books away when Bryan came by. He played football too, but he wasn't good friends with Max and therefore was more likely to be mean. He slapped my textbooks out of my hand and stared at me with eyes the size of raisins. He had stubble on his chin, which was impressive.

"Teacher's pet," he sneered.

I started to pick up my books. "I'm not sure I understand that saying," I murmured. "If you're implying that she likes me, then I hope you're right."

He kicked my books across the hall.

"You think you're so smart, don't you?" he asked.

People were watching now. One of them was Raya. I was already infatuated with her then, so it made my cheeks burn when I saw her. A few kids were laughing.

Including Taj, who was watching from down the hall.

"Not really," I said, bending down to try to get my books.

He put his right shoe on my shoulder and pushed me to the ground. I smacked my thigh on the hard ceramic tiles. Then he looked down at me, and for a second I thought he might hit me. "You're a loser," he spat. "You're a suck-up and a nobody. Enjoy your words and your As, because that's all you got."

I heard people laughing again. I shouldn't have been offended. Words and As aren't the worst things in the world, but I wanted more than that. And when you spend your days fighting Zaps and the Great Space and your nights are Routines that take three hours and leave you crying and alone, words can hurt. There was a lot of hate in his eyes that I didn't understand. Later I found out that Bryan's mom was gone and his dad drank a lot and his brother was in jail, so who can blame him for having hate in his eyes? But that day they were directed at me, and I started to well up, and I knew I was in trouble. Thankfully, Max showed up right then and pushed Bryan away and threatened to fight him, so that was that.

I scooped my books up quickly, told Max thanks, and left, trying to ignore the laughter. I ran to this field because I wanted to be alone, and stayed here until sundown, when the darkness scared me away.

"What are you thinking about?" Sara asked me.

"Nothing," I said.

She smiled. "Sure." She looked out over the field. "This is my favorite place."

"Because you can be alone?"

"Because I can imagine I could be completely alone," she corrected.

I glanced at her. "What would you do?"

She shrugged. "I don't know. Go to Times Square and do the funky chicken. Or go to the top of the Empire State Building and lie down and look at the stars. Check out London and Delhi and Rio. Maybe go into rich people's houses and pretend to be really rich for a while."

"That sounds weird."

"I don't think so," she said, almost dreamily. "Imagine the freedom."

I was a little unnerved by her voice. She almost seemed happy.

"Have you talked to your mom about John and the recording?" I asked guardedly.

"Of course not," she said. "I didn't want to before. Now I hate her. When I get John, I'll take her down too. She won't mind losing me. She probably always wanted to."

"I'm sure that's not true."

She shrugged. "Like I said, it's not easy having a crazy kid. I mean, they had to pay for a TA and they fought a lot about me and they got awkward when I was at the table and not saying anything, and sometimes I knew by her face that she wished I wouldn't be there anymore. Not like she wanted me to die or she was going to kill me or something. She just wished I wasn't there. Not like my dad."

"I . . . I don't know what to say."

"It's okay. People always want the easiest thing. That's why you touch stuff, like, a hundred times for no reason." She paused. "I read the book too."

We kept walking. She was wearing a ball cap today with her ponytail pulled through the back, along with a heavy coat pulled to her chin. I wished I had dressed a little warmer—my ears were stinging.

"Do you think I'm even crazier now?" she asked, glancing at me.

"No. The same amount of crazy."

Sara laughed. "Sweet. So, what are you going to do about the OCD?"

"I don't know. It said there are meds and therapy and stuff. But I don't want anyone to know."

"Why?"

"Because they'll treat me different," I said simply. "You know that."

She sighed and looked out at where the sky and the earth met. "Yeah." She glanced at me. "I won't. There's this thing I go to on Wednesdays. Group therapy. Open invite. It's for people with anxiety disorders."

I shook my head. "I don't think I'm ready for that."

"The people there are nice. They're all a little batty, like us."

"I don't want people to think I'm batty," I said sullenly.

She shrugged. "Suit yourself. If you ever change your mind, it's every Wednesday."

We walked for a while in silence.

"What are we going to do about John?" I asked, changing the subject.

"We almost have a case," she said thoughtfully. "But it's not ready. We might have a weapon, but we don't know anything else." She paused. "We need a body."

I felt my skin go cold. "You mean—"

"We need to find my dad," she said quietly. "There's no murder until that. Just accusations."

"How are we going to figure that out?"

"I don't know," she said. "That's the next step." She turned to me. "I know this is getting heavy. If you want out, I'll understand. You've helped me a ton, and I really appreciate it. You've done enough."

I was tempted to take her up on the offer. But I knew I couldn't.

"We'll figure something out."

She smiled. "Thanks. Want to know what I do sometimes?"

"Sure."

She suddenly took off, running like mad. I was so surprised, I just stood there for a moment, stunned. She was sprinting through a meadow of tall grass almost reaching up to her waist like she was wading in the water. Her pony-tail bounced around madly.

"Sara?" I called.

I did the only thing that made any sense: I took off after her, chasing her across the field. She was surprisingly fast.

She was halfway to the next field when she stopped, laughing and bending over. I caught up to her, doubling over myself with cramps.

"What was that about?"

She looked at me, smiling. "Freedom."

I shook my head, but we both started to laugh as we straightened up.

"You know . . . I kind of had a crush on you," she said.

"You did?"

"Yeah. A couple of years ago. I thought you were strange, but in the best kind of way."

I felt the tingling again. "Why are you telling me that?"

She shrugged. "Felt like it. Never told anyone, as you might have guessed."

"Yeah," I murmured.

She waved a hand. "Don't worry. I know you like Raya, and I have a new crush anyway."

"Who?"

She frowned. "None of your business. Now let's get back. I'll try not to act bonkers anymore."

"That would be nice."

She grabbed my hand and pulled me back toward town.

"Come on. We have a murder to solve. Try to stay focused, Daniel."

We hurried back to the road, and I tried to make sense of Sara Malvern.

CHAPTER 21

I had kind of thought that knowing what I had and being able to call it something would make it better. But when I went to bed that night, I stood in front of the mirror brushing my teeth and wondered if I could just stop it now. If I could just brush however many times I wanted and put the toothbrush away.

I looked at myself carefully. I focused on my eyes because everyone says they are the window to the soul and I wanted to know if my soul was fixed. I'm not sure if I believe in souls, of course, though I would certainly like to. Or at least I hoped my malfunctioning amygdala would stop being such a jerk.

I went to put the toothbrush down and got Zapped. I felt my insides go hard and the back of my neck tingle, and the thought went through my head that said, *I did that*

wrong and now I can't breathe and I'm going to die in my sleep.
And then my insides got worse and I started brushing my
teeth like normal.

It's funny to be a prisoner of yourself. Like you're
being bullied by your own mind and you're afraid of it,
but it's also you and it's extremely confusing. I brushed
for twenty minutes more, and when I was done, my gums
were bleeding again.

And then it was thirty minutes to leave the bathroom
and an hour at the light switch, and when I finally went to
bed, I stared at the ceiling and wondered what the point
of mental illness was. Like, if it was just that something was
broken or if they were there for a reason. Maybe I was a
Star Kid. Maybe I was special.

But when I fell asleep, I was crying again, and I didn't
feel special at all.

Monday was a strange day at school. Taj was calling me
"Dan the Man" and guys were shaking my shoulders and
shouting "State championship!" all day, which was nice
but also a bit jarring. I would come out of the bathroom,
and someone would do it. Or when I tried to eat my bologna
sandwich and Taj hit me on the back and I dropped it on
the table. I lost the slice of cheese, and it wasn't the same
after.

I ran into Sara between periods when I went to the

bathroom. By now her TA was beginning to expect that we would talk, and she just smiled at me and took out her phone. Sara stopped beside me.

"She said you must be very special to make me talk," Sara said.

I flushed. "Oh. What did you tell her?"

"I nodded. I had a nice walk yesterday."

"Me too."

She leaned in a little. "I have a plan."

I looked at her in surprise. "Already?"

"I have time," she said. "This Sunday? Can you make it?"

"I guess."

She smiled. "Good. Have fun in math."

"Thanks," I muttered.

She took off like she had never even stopped, and her TA hurried after her.

I had an even stranger encounter with Raya. We were leaving last class after the bell, and I was heading for my locker and then down to the locker room to resignedly change into practice gear. We were practicing every day leading up to the state championship, which was on Saturday morning. The Erie Hills Elephants had never won a state championship, so this was a pretty big deal to everyone but me. I had been slapped on the back twenty-one times and had talked to the team more than I had in the previous two years combined.

"Hey!" a familiar voice called out behind me.

I turned around, and my stomach did its usual flutter as Raya hurried toward me. She was wearing a wry smile. She had on a white blouse and a Technicolor shawl wrapped around her neck and dangling down to a wide leather belt. I don't know why I always noticed her clothes. I guess I tried to read her mood or intentions in them. If I had to guess today, it was that she cared about her appearance a lot for some reason, because she was extra stylish and her hair was nice.

"Hey," I said.

She stopped, her hands in her pockets. "Didn't talk to you much today."

Was that a question? "I know," I said. "I guess the football team was around a lot."

She smiled. "You're one of them now, I guess."

"Until I miss a kick and blow the championships."

"Basically."

There was a moment of silence. Was I supposed to say something else? *Think, Daniel!*

She beat me to it. "So my dad wasn't overly thrilled that he caught us kissing."

I felt my cheeks go crimson. "Oh."

"He's not going to, like, beat you up or something. He just wanted to know who you were."

"Did you give him my address?"

She laughed. "He's not a hit man. I told him it was a game. But I did tell him your name and stuff and that you aren't a jerk and that you were really embarrassed."

"All true."

"Anyway, he said he doesn't, like, ban you from my house or hanging out with me or anything."

My brain was working really hard to map this all out, but it was a lot to process.

"That's good. I guess I'll never be the outlawed bad boy of your dreams, then."

Did I just say that? She broke out laughing, and somehow her hand found her way to my arm.

"I guess not," she said. "You're stuck being the nice guy. But you're allowed around, so that's good." Her hand fell away quickly and went back to her pocket. I saw Max watching me, smirking.

"Yeah," I said, uncertain.

"See you tomorrow, Dan," she said. And then she was gone, and I was very confused.

Max appeared beside me, still wearing that knowing grin. "You look like a fire hydrant."

"I don't get girls."

He laughed and pushed me toward my locker. "Join the club."

. . .

"How?" Coach Clemons asked. "We're at the fifteen, Dan. The fifteen!"

I shrugged. "I'm just not a very good kicker, Coach."

"I am!" Kevin volunteered. We were taking turns kicking now that Kevin was back, and even though he wasn't nearly 100 percent, he was still hitting a lot more frequently than me. Unfortunately, Coach was apparently now convinced that I was a good-luck charm and insisted that I was starting on Saturday, despite both of our objections.

"You're just not focusing," Coach Clemons said. "You need to focus."

He looked like he had aged five years since play-offs had started. There were at least twice the gray hairs in his bristly mustache, and I'm pretty sure he was now balding beneath his Erie Hills ball cap. He definitely looked stressed most of the time, and there were veins on his temples that looked perilously close to bursting.

"Laps!" he shouted. "Five laps and then we try the red zone play again."

A chorus of groans went up, and I dejectedly joined the group as they started for the track. Kevin came up beside me, glancing at me with his small dark eyes and a very sour expression on his face.

"I should be playing."

"I agree."

"You stole my spot."

I looked at him. "Take it back."

"Don't play coy with me!"

"I'm serious," I said. "I hate playing. If I could go back to water boy, I would be happy."

He snarled and ran past me. I let him go. The guys here would never believe that I actually didn't want to play, and I had a feeling that Kevin was planning on taking me out somehow, so I was going to stay clear of him. As much as I didn't want to play, I didn't want to get beat up either.

As we ran, I saw Coach going over some plays with the assistant coach, yelling and spitting and just generally going crazy. It was funny how seriously they all took football. No one seemed to care about the other things going on when practice ended.

"Rough practice," Max said, appearing beside me.

"I know."

"You'll be fine. You're two for two. One more play, and we're there."

I frowned. "Yeah. Is your dad coming to watch—"

"Yeah. Called last night. Said he wouldn't miss the state championship."

I could see Max clenching his fists as he ran. I knew he would be crazed all week again.

"We'll win," I said.

Max smiled. "That's the spirit. You have a fan, by the way."

I followed his gaze and saw Sara waiting by the school, watching us run.

"Two girls now?" Max asked me. "Who are you? What did you do with Dan?"

I shook my head resignedly. "I have no idea."

CHAPTER 22

It turned out that Sara's mom was just late picking Sara up. Sara had been sitting alone in the front and had decided to come watch us practice. We went back to the front to wait for her mom, and even though I saw some of the guys grinning and shooting me weird looks as they rode away with their parents, I didn't leave. I guess I was trying so hard to be a decent football player that I was too tired to try to be cool, too.

In any case, we sat there on the curb and talked as the sun headed toward the hills.

"I don't even really want rides from her," Sara said, "for obvious reasons. But it's a bit of a far walk. I mean, if we end up proving John's guilt and she's involved, then I guess I'll have to figure it out."

I paused. "What would happen to you?"

"I don't know," she said. "I'm thirteen, so I guess I would become legal custody of my grandparents. Except I'm not sure they want me either. They're nice, but that doesn't mean they want a kid on antidepressant medication living there. No one does, really. So maybe foster care or something."

I watched as Tom Dernt rode away, watching me with a raised eyebrow.

"Maybe your mom had nothing to do with it."

"I hope so. But it didn't sound like it. And to be honest, she and my dad fought a lot."

I glanced at her. "About you?"

"And other things. They fought about how much she worked and how she went out a lot, and sometimes about his drinking. He drank sometimes. But he was a good dad. Trust me."

"You never said he drank."

She shrugged. "He wasn't, like, a raging drunk or anything."

I didn't want to say it, but I guess I had to. "And you're definitely sure he didn't just run away?"

She looked at me, her green eyes flashing. "Yes," she said coldly. "Besides all the evidence we have been gathering, I just know he didn't. He loved me, Dan. He was in my room every night reading to me and tucking me in and telling me he loved me. He would never have left me.

Never. And if you even have to think that still, then maybe you shouldn't be helping me after all."

The sharpness in her voice caught me off guard. "I'm sorry."

She shook her head, not saying anything. For a minute or two we sat in silence as the rest of the team took off. Coach Clemons was last, and he just gave me a suspicious look like I should have been at home studying the playbook or something, even though my job was just to kick the ball sometimes.

"I miss him," she said.

"I know."

"He didn't leave me, Dan. He knew my . . . condition. The panic attacks and the depression. He wouldn't have left me."

I put my hand on her knee. "I believe you." I felt her leg twitch, and I pulled away.

"Sorry," she murmured. "Don't get touched much. Here. Look." She pulled out her cell phone and opened the gallery. She scrolled through endless pictures of her and her dad—at the beach, hugging, hiking, at a dinner party, and just sitting together on the couch. I saw a lot of her dad in her: the green eyes and the dark hair. In every picture he was smiling and jovial and had his arm around her shoulders.

"Did you talk to him?" I asked quietly.

"Yes," she whispered. "He was the only one in the world. Until you."

I nodded. "He looks happy."

She smiled sadly. "He was. That's what I mean. There's no way he ran."

I nodded. "I guess so. But you said it yourself. There is no record of a murder. We need a body."

"I told you . . . I have a plan."

"That usually gets us into trouble."

"And this will probably be no exception," she said.

I sighed. "Figured."

A blue sedan suddenly sped into the parking lot, and I recognized Sara's mom at the wheel. She waved at me, and Sara rolled her eyes.

"You want a ride?"

I shook my head. "I'll walk. Could use the fresh air."

What I really meant was that I didn't want to be in the car with Sara's mother, since we were planning a way to get her and her boyfriend arrested for murder.

"Suit yourself," she said. "See you tomorrow."

"Bye."

They drove away, and I started the walk home alone.

My dad got off work early that night, so we had dinner as a family. Steve of course wasn't a fan of that, but my dad was there, so Steve had to show up and behave anyway.

We even had pizza, which was usually our Saturday night routine. For a Monday it was unheard of.

My mom turned to Emma. "How was your day, dear?"

She shrugged. "Good. Had a test."

"A?" Steve asked dryly.

"Probably," she said.

"How about you, Steve?" my dad asked.

"Day was good."

"He means the grades," my mom said.

"No tests," he said. "I'm passing everything."

"Now that's something to strive for," my dad said sarcastically.

"Dan?" my mom asked.

"Fine."

"How was practice?" Dad asked.

"Same as usual. Missed a bunch until the coach yelled at me."

Steve snickered.

"It's the game that counts," my dad said. "You just need to—"

"Focus," I finished. "I know."

He nodded and went back to his pizza. Next to me Emma was nibbling on a cheese slice like a mouse, while Steve wolfed down the rest of the pizza on the other side. My mom had her eyes on me, and I slid my hand away from where I was moving my milk glass back and forth across the table. Eight times. I needed two more, but I could wait until she looked away again. As soon as she did, I snuck in two more moves and finally relaxed. I had left the pizza on the plate while I'd been doing it. When I was Zapped, the first thing to go was my appetite.

"How is everything else?" my mom asked. Her voice had changed a little. I wondered if she had seen the milk glass. Sometimes I thought she saw little things like that, but I was never sure.

"Fine," I said.

She nodded. "Sleeping okay? I heard you moving around last night."

My cheeks were burning now. I definitely wasn't going to eat. "Fine. Restless, I guess."

She stared at me for a moment. Why did she have to ask me in front of everyone?

"So how is Sara?" she said.

I glanced at her. "Fine . . ."

"I haven't seen her around here in a bit. Do you still hang out?"

Emma was watching me now, smiling coyly. My dad was watching with equal interest.

"Yeah," I said. "Sometimes."

"What do you do?" Steve asked through a mouthful of pizza.

"Steve," she said. "Not with your mouth full. But what do you do? Does she . . . talk much?"

I sighed. "What have you heard?"

She gave me an innocent look. "I just heard from one of the moms that she's . . . quiet."

"I heard she's nuts," Steve said.

I wasn't one to react much, especially where my brother was concerned. He was older and bigger, and I had grown up terrified of him. But I felt my temper rising.

"She is not nuts," I said sharply.

He wasn't intimidated. "They call her Psycho Sara."

"It's not nice," Emma murmured.

My mom looked caught between rebuking Steve and wanting to ask me if it was true. I decided to save her the trouble. "They call her that because she doesn't like to talk much. And since the other kids spend their time calling her Psycho Sara, can you blame her? She's actually a genius, if you must know."

My mom and dad exchanged a surprised look. I was a little shocked myself.

"Can I be excused?"

My mom nodded. "Sure. Steve?"

"Sorry," he muttered.

I just left my pizza half-eaten on the plate and stormed up to my room, closed the door, and flopped onto my bed. I felt the heat in my cheeks and the back of my neck and was still wondering where that had come from. I knew everyone called her Psycho Sara. I even knew they were probably whispering about the fact that I was hanging out with her now. But I felt strangely protective of her. Like she had showed me who she really was, and now I was tasked with defending her. Not that she needed it.

Another thought suddenly occurred to me. Did I like Sara Malvern? It didn't even make any sense. I liked Raya. Cool, normal, popular Raya Singh, who reminded me of what I wanted to be—normal too. Sara was the world I wanted to get away from. The crazy one where our minds didn't work right and we chased murderers and I tried to figure out a girl who made no sense.

I wanted to just like Raya Singh and leave it there. But as I stared up at the stucco ceiling, it wasn't Raya's face I saw there.

I ended up writing a few more chapters before bed. I was finally getting the rhythm. I wrote a few flashbacks and "character building" scenes, like the day Daniel fought with his mom and the day his grandpa died. Then I got to the gas station scene.

They pulled into a gas station standing alone at the side of the highway. Its neon sign was still shining brightly in the gloomy midday light. They stopped in front of the pump.

"I'll fill it," she said. "You make sure it's all clear."

"Split up?" he said weakly.

"Unless you're too afraid."

Daniel sighed. "Fine."

He grabbed the baseball bat and started for the side of the building. He peered into the store through the glass, but it was abandoned. He crept around the side, peeking into the back parking lot.

"Sara, you almost done?" he called nervously.

"I haven't even started."

"Oh."

He spotted the bathroom door and realized he kind of had to go. He glanced at Sara. It would probably be another minute or so before she filled the tank. He had some time. Dan tried the door and found that it was open. Taking a quick look inside, he hurried in.

After washing his hands, he pushed the door open, the bat hanging lazily from his other hand. The creature was waiting.

It towered over him, its black, vacant eyes locked on his. Then it raised one of its terrible, clawed hands and prepared to bring it down on Daniel's head.

The baseball bat dropped from his hands. He was too afraid to move.

And then a croquet mallet swung past him and connected squarely with the creature's head. There was a burst of electric blue light and a *boom,* and the creature went sailing backward into the trees lining the parking lot.

Sara turned to him. "Shall we go?"

They ran to the car and jumped in just as two more creatures started running toward the source of the noise. Sara floored the gas pedal, and they sped out onto the street.

Daniel looked at her, amazed.

She just smiled. "I told you it wasn't a normal croquet mallet. Now try to hold it, if you can. We have a world to save, and it's going to be tough if you get killed going to the bathroom before we get there."

Game day was bright and sunny. Perfect kicking conditions, which meant I had no excuse if I messed it up. My mom woke me up by flinging my curtains open.

"Big game today," she said.

Then she left me in the sunlight, and I tried to burrow back under my blankets. I tried to think of some viable excuses. Flu? They wouldn't buy it. I could fake an injury. Maybe a fall off the front porch?

I had three bites of cereal, and by the third bite my Mini-Wheats were soggy and looked like porridge. I tossed the rest and went to the bathroom to stare at the toilet for a while in case I got sick. There was no vomiting, though, and instead I moved to the mirror to reflect that I was looking rather pale. Maybe the flu wouldn't be so far-fetched after all. My hair was standing on end, but I just threw a ball cap on and started downstairs, where my dad was waiting to drive me. He looked excited.

He gave me a rare pat on the back.

"Ready?"

"Yeah," I murmured.

He grinned. "Nerves are good."

I managed a weak smile and followed him to the car. I walked off the porch and totally forgot to fake a fall. I was stuck playing now. My stomach twisted a little more. The drive to the field was the longest ever. My dad was talking about plays and the wind and the sun, but I was just thinking that I should have taken up drama or something. I was definitely going to blow the game today. It was just a matter of time.

The Rocanville Ravens were already warming up on the field. They wore all black, which didn't help the dread sweeping over me. It looked like we were playing a team of wraiths or something. This was not cool.

Before I knew it, the whistle had blown and I was kicking the ball as hard as I could toward the waiting Ravens. It was a decent connection, and Coach even patted my back on my way off the field.

"That's it, Leigh," he said, sounding like he was about to explode with pent-up energy.

It was the end of the first quarter when I attempted my

first field goal. We were down three—the defense on both teams was shutting down the offense. I trotted out, trying to ignore Raya and my dad and the hundred other people watching me.

"Hut!"

Max caught the ball and placed it perfectly. Laces out. I kicked.

It sailed left by about five yards and plopped into the end zone. I had missed. I saw Max bite his lip, but then he stood up, and shook my hand, and said, "Next time, baby."

Coach ignored me on my way back to the bench, and I found a spot and slumped. Bad start. It was a close game. Tom was throwing well, and as usual Max was finding his way to the score sheet. He had two touchdowns by the half, and we were down by seven.

Coach Clemons's halftime speech was mostly yelling.

"We're right in it, boys!" he screamed, spittle flying from his mouth and showering poor Brayden Little. "A little more work on D, and we have it. Leigh, stay focused, son! You can do this, Dan!"

I'd already missed another field goal and an extra point, so I was one for four at the moment. Most of the other guys weren't even looking at me, and I was afraid to check the stands. My family was probably hiding their faces. It was just as bad as I had feared. I was blowing the game.

I missed another field goal in the third quarter. Kevin

was making a lot of loud comments from the sidelines about how I should be replaced, but Coach wasn't having it. We were still only a touchdown behind, so I guess he figured I was still good luck or something. It didn't feel like it as I watched another ball sail wide. I did sneak a quick look at my dad on my way back to the sidelines, and he gave me the fakest smile ever and clapped. He'd never been much of an actor. Even Emma looked uncomfortable.

I watched in horror as the game stayed close into the fourth quarter. When Max tied the game with ten minutes left, the bench went crazy. I stayed where I was, feeling my insides churn. It was too close. It was going to come down to me. I already knew it. And I was going to miss.

It felt like the game was happening in slow motion. A few minutes later I saw Taj crunch into a running back. Kyle sacked their quarterback. Before I knew it, they were punting, and we were back on our ten.

There were five minutes left, and we were all tied.

I stood up and watched the drive, feeling my hands and knees trembling with every yard. I just needed Max to score again. We would win with the touchdown, and it wouldn't matter. For a second it looked like I would get my wish. He caught a long fly and was breaking for the end zone when they brought him down. A minute left. They would take a few more chances.

The first down was a loss of two. Then we gained five. Third down.

I was biting my nails as Tom caught the ball and dropped back, scanning the field. They were double teaming Max by now, but he was still too quick. He cut inside, leaving the defenders for just a moment, and Tom stepped into the pass, throwing a perfect spiral.

And then Max dropped it. I don't think I'd ever seen him drop a pass before. He just let it thud solidly into his chest, and then it bounced inexorably out again through his outstretched fingers.

It was silent on the bench. In the stands, too. I watched in disbelief as Max stared down at the ball and then his fingers. He couldn't believe it either.

Coach Clemons turned to me, his face white. "You're up, Leigh."

It was like a funeral procession as I ran out to the field. We'd been stopped at the thirty-one—in my range but still a hefty kick. I had never been so nervous in my life. I could barely stop my right leg from twitching as I stopped in the huddle. Max was still too stunned to speak. I patted his helmet.

"It's okay, man," I said.

He looked at me and nodded. I knew what he was thinking—*You're going to miss and we're going to lose.* I felt like I was about to faint. I stupidly looked at the stands and saw my parents holding hands. Steve and Emma watched nervously.

Raya was with Clara, and they were holding each other around the shoulders. Everyone stared at me.

The team lined up. Max took his position. I stepped back and swallowed down some acid reflux.

It was quiet. Neither set of fans wanted to speak. And then I saw her.

She was watching from behind the field goalpost, leaning against a tree with her leg propped up. My stomach did one last little flop. Even Sara was watching. Everyone I knew was there.

And then I noticed she was holding something. A sign. She turned to face me, smiled, and put the sign in front of her. It read:

FOOTBALL SUCKS

I laughed. I couldn't help it. The sound burst out with a nervous, pent-up energy that split through the silence. She just stood there, holding the sign and leaning against the tree like it was a perfectly normal thing to do. I kept my eyes on her.

"Hut!"

The ball flew back, and Max placed it. I didn't even think about it. It was just a game.

I swung through and connected as cleanly as I ever had. As the ball left my cleat, I knew the kick was good. The ball sailed through the goalposts, and everything became a mess of noise and jumping and laughter. I was picked up and carried to the sidelines, and Max wrapped me in a hug, almost crying, he was so happy. I remember ribbons and a trophy and my dad telling me he was proud, but most of all I remember Sara, standing against the tree with the sign and watching it all with a smile.

CHAPTER 23

Winning the state championship was a pretty big deal, I guess, since we all went out for lunch and got ice cream, and my dad even drank a beer, which he never does. It felt like the whole rest of the day was a flurry of activity, all the way to the barbecue at Coach's house that night that went until ten.

When I got home, I was exhausted, but I'd managed to have almost a full day without any Zaps—or obsessions, I think they're called—and that was pretty nice. I felt as happy as I had in a long time when I got to my room and sat down at my computer. I thought for a second I might even be able to skip the Routine, but I knew the second I thought it that I would never be able to. Right away I felt ill.

It was okay. I would just delay it a little. I opened Facebook and looked at pictures from the game for a while. Some of the guys had posted them, and I was even tagged in one. That was the first time that had ever happened.

I wasn't even thinking about my cell phone. When I finally decided to go to bed, I checked it out of habit, and froze. There were five missed calls. All from Sara's cell phone. And all of them were from an hour or two before. Frowning, I called the number back.

Sara's mom answered immediately. She sounded panicked.

"Is this Daniel?"

"Yeah."

"Is Sara with you?"

"No," I said. "Why?"

I heard her mom stifle a sob. "She's gone. I haven't seen her all day. Her phone was here. She's gone."

I was too stunned to say anything for a moment. Then I asked, "When was the last time you saw her?"

"After she got home from your game. We . . . got into a fight. I mean, as much as we can fight when she barely talks to me. She wanted to leave. She wanted to go to the library, and I wanted to drive her, but she wouldn't let me. But it's too far to walk. John gave her a ride. He said he dropped her off. But the library didn't see her. They know her. She was never there."

I felt my insides go cold. "John drove her?"

"Yeah. He's out looking for her now. I called the police."

I looked at the window. "I'm going to go look for her myself."

I didn't wait to hear what she said. I shoved the phone into my pocket and hurried downstairs.

I searched all through the night. My mom went with me and drove me around for a while, but there was nothing. It was dark, and we found nothing but shadows. We drove in silence.

It was almost two when my mom drove me home.

"I'm sorry, Dan," she said. "There's nothing we can do tonight. The police are looking."

"I think it was her mother's boyfriend," I said.

She looked at me. "What?"

"We've been investigating him. Sara thinks he killed her dad. She might have confronted him. If she did, he might have done something to her." It was all rushing out now. "She could be in danger."

My mom frowned. "Why would you even think that? Do you have any proof?"

"We have our reasons."

She looked at me. "I'll call the police station. They're going to want to talk with you."

I nodded. "Call."

They were at the house ten minutes later. Two of them—a young man with a goatee and big arms and an older, graying sergeant with a big gut and unfriendly eyes. They sat across from me in the kitchen.

I was careful to hide some of the details—namely the whole breaking-and-entering part. But I told them about the recorded message and the apology John gave her and the fake note that was written by John.

They looked at each other a few times, and my mom and dad watched from the kitchen.

"We can go talk to John," the older one, Sergeant Bent, said gruffly. "But we can't arrest anyone based on notes and apologies. I know John. Not a bad guy. We'll go talk to him, though."

The younger officer turned to me. "Her mom said the girl doesn't talk to anyone but you. Why?"

I paused. "I don't know. I guess she knew I would listen."

They glanced at each other again and went to talk to my parents in hushed voices. They didn't believe me. That was obvious. And I didn't care, but I cared about Sara.

"Who's looking for Sara?" I asked loudly.

Sergeant Bent turned to me. "We have three officers out now. They'll find her, kid. She's fine."

Then they left, and my parents came back and told me to go to bed. They didn't believe me either.

My mom kissed me on the forehead and whispered, "She'll be fine. You'll see her in the morning."

Then she left with my dad, and I was alone in my room again. I paced for a while. I wanted to do the Routine to feel better, but I wasn't ready to go to bed. All I could think about was Sara. What if he had done something to her? I sat down and stood up and wondered what to do.

How could I sleep when she was out there?

I thought back over the last few weeks. The day in the hallway. The touch game. The sign. The trips to John's. The night in the bushes. The walk through the field, when she told me she wanted to be alone.

I was out the door before my parents had even gone to bed.

"Sara?"

I was walking through the blackness, the grass up to my waist. It was like wading through the water at night, the only light the endless stars overhead and the streetlights behind me. It was cold, and I felt it slithering under my sweater and jeans and clinging to my skin like a wet towel. I shivered.

"Sara!"

"I'm here," a faint voice replied, barely carrying even in the silence.

I found her a minute later. She was lying flat on her

back, sunken right down in the grass. She was just staring up at the sky, not even moving when I appeared over her.

"Hey," I said.

"Hey."

I crouched down next to her, frowning. "Everyone is looking for you."

She kept her eyes on the stars. "I guess that makes sense."

"How long have you been here?"

She paused. "I don't know. I don't have my phone. Since lunch, I guess."

I stared at her for a moment, and then lay down in the grass. It was cold and damp and kind of weird to submerge myself in the darkness, but sometimes you do strange things for other people.

I guess that's friendship.

"How is lying in the middle of a field at nighttime?" she asked.

"Different."

The stars were beautiful, just visible through the wisps of blackness extending all around my vision like at the edges of a black hole.

She laughed. "Yeah. I'm sorry you looked for me. I should have gone home."

"Why didn't you? What happened today?"

"I fought with my mom. She told me she was trying

her best to take care of me by herself. I told her that it was her fault she was by herself. That I missed Dad. That I wished I had gone with him instead."

"You *said* that?"

"Yeah. She started to cry. Told me I didn't know anything about it. John intervened. He offered to drive me to the library. I agreed. I wanted to talk to him anyway. Took him by surprise, as you can imagine."

I glanced at her. I could only make out the gentle lines of her face in the darkness, and the stars reflecting in her eyes. "And?"

"I asked him if he knew my dad. He said no. I asked him if he knew where my dad was. He said no. I asked him if he had any regrets about the way everything happened."

She fell silent.

"And?" I asked.

"He looked at me and said yes. And he said he was sorry. But he wouldn't say anything else."

We listened to the crickets for a while.

"I told the cops that I thought John did something to you."

She looked at me. "What?"

"They came over, and I told them everything. Well, not the breaking-into-John's-house and stuff, but everything else."

"And they didn't believe you."

"How do you know that?"

"Because I already wrote them a letter. They told me they can't do anything without proof."

I sighed. "So we don't have enough."

"No. But he basically admitted it to me tonight. So I came here. I couldn't look at them."

I reached out and found her hand in the darkness. It was cold and clammy. Our shoulders were pressed together tightly, and there was just enough heat there to keep me from shivering. But she must have been very cold by now.

"We should go back," I said quietly.

"Five minutes?"

I smiled. "Sure."

We lay there in silence for a while, and then started the walk home.

CHAPTER 24

Sara's mom ran out screaming and crying, and hugged her until Sara had to pry her off. She just nodded at her mom and John and the police officer who was there and went upstairs. It was up to me to answer the questions, but I just said she'd run away and I'd found her in a place where she liked to hide.

They asked me more questions, but I said I was tired, and they eventually let me go.

John offered to drive me, but I said no and walked.

My parents didn't even notice I'd been gone. I crept back into the house and went to my room and started the Routine at four in the morning. I got to bed at five and fell asleep immediately.

I woke up to an email from Sara.

Today is the day. Meet me at the corner by John's house
at 2 p.m.

I rolled over and tried to go back to sleep. But it was
too late. The sun was shining through the windows, and
we were going to try to catch a murderer later. I climbed
out of bed.

I ate breakfast with Emma. Luckily, my parents had
slept in after the late night. I didn't want to have a talk
about false accusations and my crazy friend Sara and whatever else was in store.

"I was listening last night," Emma said.

I sighed. "To how much?"

"All of it."

I looked at her in annoyance. "It was, like, one in the
morning."

"I was reading," she said innocently. "I just over-
heard it."

"Sure."

She put her spoon down and looked at me thoughtfully. "You're investigating a murder."

"Sort of."

She nodded, as if this was perfectly normal news. She
tapped her finger on the table.

"Have you found a weapon?"

I frowned. "Maybe."

"Motive?"

"I think so."

She nodded. "But you clearly don't have a body."

"How do you know to ask all this?" I asked, scowling.

"*CSI.*"

"Mom told you to stop watching *CSI.*"

She shrugged. "Well, if you don't have a body, you need a confession. Or you need the culprit to lead you to the body. You have circumstantial evidence, and that just won't do."

I stared at her, rubbing my forehead in exasperation. "You watch too much TV."

"And you should have recruited me from the beginning," she said sullenly. "What are you doing today anyway?"

I pushed my bowl away and leaned back. "Probably trying to get a confession."

Before I went to meet Sara, I decided to write a little more. I was freaked out about going back to John's, and I thought writing might calm me down a little. Besides, I figured authors wrote even when they didn't really want to, including days when they had to go solve a murder. I guess. I didn't really know any authors.

I did know that I was very close to having a panic attack, which I had learned about from the book. It should have made me feel better to know about the real thing, but it didn't. Writing did, though. Normal Daniel still lived in there.

I had written a few more chapters since the gas station . . . mostly short ones. It was going to be a short novel, I guess. Maybe a novella at best. But I could always add more later.

I had just reached the part when they got to the New York apartment building. It was getting exciting. They were almost to the switch.

Sara and Dan crept up the stairs, the silence heavy in the twenty-story concrete staircase. It hadn't been easy narrowing it down to this Charles Oliver, and it had nearly cost them their lives visiting the last two apartments. But this time they were almost sure: even his home voice mail had said, "Charles Oliver . . . if this is an emergency, call me directly. If you can't . . . then you better come up and fix it."

They could have used the elevator, but Sara said if it opened and there was a monster in front of them, they were in serious trouble. She preferred the stairs.

And so they climbed one silent step after another, and the bat trembled in Daniel's hands. He was afraid, but he was eager to finally get there. He could almost fix his mistake.

They reached the ninth floor and stepped out into the hallway. It was eerily quiet.

They looked both ways. Nothing. Sara nodded at Dan and started down the hallway, moving like a prowling cat. Dan followed, feeling his skin crawl. It was too quiet.

They were almost to the apartment when he looked back and saw it.

They weren't alone.

A creature was watching them from the other end of the hall, stretching its fingers out like it was getting ready to feast. Daniel turned to Sara.

"Run!"

They sprinted down the hall and skidded to a halt in front of 912. Sara knocked.

"Remember how everyone is gone?" Dan asked.

The creature was walking toward them, its claws extended.

"Right," she said. "So, what are we going to do?"

He looked at her. "I thought you had a plan?"

"No."

The creature was almost to them. He could see the light reflecting off its claws. Sara turned to the doorknob. "Apartments usually have a door lock and a dead bolt."

Daniel's eyes widened as the creature locked its eyes on him. "Do it!"

Sara swung her croquet mallet around and aimed it at the handle. There was a flash of blue, and the knob went rolling across the floor. She kicked the door opened and they raced inside. They closed it just in time. There was a thump on the other side, and they both pressed their backs to the door as Sara fumbled with the dead bolt and locked it.

I sat back and looked at the time. Sara was waiting. It was time to go solve this murder once and for all.

We met at the corner of John's street. It was a brisk, clear November day; just cold enough to bite at the tips of my nose and fingers and send a chill into my toes. Sara was waiting patiently, tucked into a clump of hedges on the corner in case John drove by.

I peaked at his house, where his black truck was parked in the driveway.

"I know," I said. "I'm late."

She shrugged. "A few minutes. No big deal."

I looked at her suspiciously. "What did you do?"

She smiled. "I took this." She fished a cell phone out of her pocket; a black iPhone that definitely wasn't hers. She unlocked it, and a picture of her smiling mother appeared on the screen.

"Where is your mom?"

"Away with my grandma. They took a shopping trip to the city. Out of touch all day. She already called from my grandma's phone to ask if she forgot her cell. She didn't; I took it from her purse earlier."

I frowned. "And the plan is . . ."

"To become my mother," she said. "My phone is in the back of John's truck. With the theft protection app on."

"You're tracking him."

"Right. Step into my office."

Sighing, I followed her into the hedge, out of sight of the road. We sat down there in the dirt. I really hoped the homeowners didn't find us perched in their shrubbery. It would be tough to explain.

Sara opened the cell phone. "We may have to move quickly. Are you ready?"

"I guess."

She nodded and started to type. *Sara is asking me questions. I think she knows.*

We waited for a minute in silence. And then the phone went off.

How? What kind of questions?

We met eyes. She typed again. *About why we did it. About you. She wants to see your house, and I think she is getting suspicious about where he is.*

What are you going to do?

Sara smiled. *Just make sure the house is clear. It's better if we let her see it. There's nothing there, right?*

Pause. *Just the letter you sent me. I can get rid of it. And if she sees my gun . . . I'll hide it.*

Good. I'll bring her by later when I'm back.

Okay.

I felt my heart thumping against my chest. It was real. All of it. I looked at her, and she went in for the kill.

If she finds anything . . . Can you make sure the spot is okay? She could find it. She's too smart.

"You just had to add that part?" I said dryly. She shrugged.

Okay. I'll go now.

Sara and I looked at each other.

"Whoa," I murmured.

"Yeah," she said quietly.

Her hands were shaking now. I understood why. Her father really was dead. Her mother had helped her boyfriend kill him. I knew Sara had always hoped she was wrong. But she wasn't. Her dad was dead, and she was about to destroy her last remaining family.

"Are you okay?" I asked.

She nodded. "There's no time for this. Stay out of sight."

It was a few minutes before an engine roared to life. We stayed low as the black truck went speeding down the road and whipped around the corner. We listened to it fade away in the distance.

"You have it?" I asked.

Sara opened her iCloud, and we saw a little blue dot driving away. "Got it." She looked at me. "There's a letter from my mom in there. We need it. We need all the evidence we can get, to be sure."

I sighed. "I'll go. Keep an eye on the GPS."

She squeezed my hand, pressing the key into my grip. "Thank you. Be quick."

I took off out of the hedge and hurried down the street, trying to look inconspicuous as two people walked by with their dog on the other side of the street. When they were past, I half-walked, half-jogged up to the porch, looked both ways, and opened the door. The familiar scent of sweat and beer hung in the air; dusty light filtered in through closed curtains. I needed to search for the letter—fast.

I checked the garbage in the kitchen first, in case he'd thrown it out. There was nothing but rotting food and wrappers. I doubted he'd taken the time to bury it in there. I continued on to the bathroom. Nothing.

He must not have thrown it out yet. I was just starting for the bedroom when I noticed the gun sitting on the hallway table. It was the one from the dresser drawer. Obviously he had taken that out to hide it and was going to make sure the body was concealed first. I felt my stomach flop. Was her father buried somewhere in the woods? Was John hiding it with brush right now? Would he do the same thing to Sara and me if he found us? Of course he would. I had to hurry.

I headed into his room, scanning the filthy space for somewhere I hadn't searched yet.

I didn't need to look far. It was obvious that John had started the process before the warning about the body. There was a letter sitting on the bed—crumpled up and written in messy pen. I slowly crossed the room, my whole body tingling, and picked up the note. The ink was stained with blotchy tears.

Dear John,

I know I shouldn't ask this of you. We've only been together for a few months, and it's been wonderful, but you don't owe me anything. But I have to ask. Things have gotten bad. Really bad. I know I haven't been a good wife or a good person and I deserve what I get. But he's always angry. Yelling when Sara is not around. He keeps drinking more and more and taking pills, and I'm afraid something is going to happen. I can't have him there anymore. Sara is starting to hear things. It's not healthy for her. She can't know about this.

I need your help. I need him out of my life. I want to start new with you, to move past this. I can't do it alone. I'm not strong enough. You don't owe me anything, but if you do this, we can finally start our lives together. So I need your help and I need you to write a note . . . a letter . . . explaining that he's gone. From him. I need something to give my darling. She still loves her father. She doesn't see him for what he has become.

I wanted to give you a letter because I can't say any of this without crying. I feel like a failed mother and wife and every-thing else. I'm sorry to bring you into this. Call me later if you'll help me.

Love,
Michelle

I read the letter slowly. It was a murder—plain and simple. We had the evidence now.

And now I had to get out of there. Fast.

I turned to go, my hands shaking on the lined sheet of paper so much that it was crackling. I think I saw the shadow before I saw the man. He was looming in the door-way, his head and broad shoulders touching the sides like a perfectly sized portrait. He was holding a gun in his right hand. The gun.

He looked at me, almost reluctantly, his eyes darker than the room.

"This is very unfortunate," he said quietly.

CHAPTER 25

I was completely frozen to the spot. The funny thing is, it felt like a Zap. My heart was beating and my breathing wasn't right and my arms were tingling. I was thinking that I was going to die, and that was the same too. The only difference was I couldn't fix it. I couldn't do anything at all except stare at the man who was about to kill me. I just had to surrender, I guess.

John held my eyes as his arm moved. And then he laid the gun on the dresser.

I looked at it, confused. He sat down on the bed, looking exhausted. He put his face in his hands.

"I didn't want to get involved in this," he said.

He wasn't even asking why I was in his house. I guess he already knew.

"She asked me, and I love her. But I always liked Sara.

I know she doesn't talk and she has her . . . issues, but I didn't mind that she was quiet. She seemed like a good kid. Her mom showed me her grades even . . . straight As. Bright girl. I thought she deserved the truth, but I trusted her mom."

I heard footsteps, and then Sara appeared in the doorway. She looked at me, confused.

"I tried to warn you," she said. "Your phone is off."

I picked up my cell phone and checked it. "Oh."

John met her eyes, and I was surprised to see that his eyes were watery. "I figured out it was you. I wasn't thinking. Your mom is gone today. And she doesn't even use caps or anything. Doesn't text much, I guess. She would have called. I was halfway there when I realized."

"Why did you do it?" Sara asked. Her eyes were glassy now too. She had her hands on the phone, ready to dial 911. Her finger was hovering over the call button. She was prepared to turn him in.

He shook his head. "She asked me to. I wasn't comfortable with it, but she said it was the best. With his condition. And when the news came in, she knew it would be too much for you. It was only a day or two later. In the hotel. She went to the police and had them hush it up. Everything was low-key. We decided to run with it."

Sara and I exchanged a confused look.

"She went to the police?"

John frowned. "Of course. She didn't want it in the paper or anything. And she knew you might go into the police station and she asked them not to say anything."

Sara leaned against the doorframe, and I thought the cell phone was about to fall out of her limp fingers. It was too much for her. I could see her trembling and her eyes fogging over, and I knew the Great Space was coming. But she needed answers.

"Why would the police cover it up?" she whispered, like she was very far away.

"They agreed it was for the best. And your mom asked, Sara. She has a right, I guess. But me . . . I had issues with my old man. Lots. I thought you deserved the truth. You deserved to mourn him."

"Mourn him?" she asked, anger flashing in her eyes now. "You killed him, and you want me to mourn him?"

John looked at her. Now he was the one who looked confused. I kept my eyes on the gun. If it went bad, I had to get there before John could. I didn't know what I would do with it, but I had to be first.

"Kill him?" he asked, bewildered. "I didn't kill anyone."

I decided to jump in. I raised the letter. "Then what is this?"

"The note she wrote me," he said, still looking baffled. "Asking me to help escort him from the house to the hotel.

And to write the letter that said he was going away. He was in no condition to do it."

Sara slid down to the floor. I wanted to help her, but none of it made any sense.

"But the gun . . ."

John turned to me. "It's a gun. Lots of people have them. I just didn't want Sara to find it and think I was a criminal or something. I have a checkered past, I'll admit. But I've changed. I wanted her to like me." He turned back to Sara. "I hoped one day she would think of me like a dad."

Sara started to cry. "A dad?" she managed. "How could you ever think that—"

John looked heartbroken. "Sara, I didn't kill him. Your dad was ill. He was severely depressed, and when he found out about your mom and me, it was too much. He was drinking and taking prescription pills, and he was in a bad place. We asked him to leave the house for a bit. To stay in a hotel. I shouldn't have been involved, but your mom couldn't do it. She had loved him. It had just been bad for a long time. It doesn't excuse me, I know. But he went to the hotel. And two days later they found him. Overdose. He killed himself."

Sara started to sob. Now I went to her and wrapped my arms around her shoulders and let her cry. Her whole body was shaking.

"Then where were you going just now?" I asked.

John wiped his eyes gruffly. "To the cemetery. I wanted to put some fresh flowers there so it looked nice if Michelle decided to tell her. I wanted her to know that we hadn't forgotten him."

"And the watch?"

He smiled faintly. "I took it. I have a friend who refinishes jewelry. I wanted to have it polished and fixed for her. I thought it would be a good gift. I don't know. I messed up, Sara. I'm sorry."

"What about the assault charge?" I asked. "What about the guy who was here to collect five thousand dollars?"

John looked at me, frowning. "You guys were here for that, too?"

"Yeah," I murmured.

"An old buddy," he said gruffly. "I won't lie, I made some bad choices earlier in my life. I hung out with some bad people, and I'm finally getting it organized now. I told your mom," he said, looking at Sara. "I wanted to change. I was trying. I even thought maybe I could have a family of my own. That's why I was willing to go along with everything. I thought maybe I could be like a dad for you eventually."

He suddenly didn't look like the man I'd thought he was. He had tattoos and a grizzled face, but his dark eyes were soft, and tears still leaked down his cheeks. His big calloused hands fidgeted in front of him.

And I knew it was true. All of it. He had really been trying to protect her.

Sara looked up through tear-dampened bangs. "Why didn't she want to tell me?"

He hesitated. But I guess he was tired of lying.

"Because he had the same thing you do, sweetie. He was depressed. Same meds even. I guess she didn't want you to think you were destined for the same fate. You aren't. You're a strong girl. Smart. She was going to tell you eventually. But she was afraid it would make you worse. That you'd never recover."

The tears streamed down her face again.

John didn't even move. He just let her sit there, crying.

We went to the cemetery later. Sara stood there for a long time staring at the headstone. There were flowers laid out beneath it, though they were withering just a little.

"I wanted to put fresh ones there," John said quietly. He didn't say anything else.

It was a nice place, I guess. I went to a cemetery once when my grandma died, and it was rainy that day and gray and everyone was crying. Today it was bright, and even in November the grass was still green and neatly cut. I saw a few other families walking around, holding hands and remembering.

It wasn't a bad place, but I don't think Sara cared. She

just needed to say good-bye. I was glad she was getting the chance.

I stood a little ways back until she turned to me and took my hand. She looked at John.

"I'm glad you got him a headstone," she said quietly. "I could read here, maybe."

He nodded. "Your mom did all that. She told me the funeral was quiet. She was here with just her mom and your dad's parents. Not me."

"He probably appreciated that," she said, looking at the headstone. "I'm sorry I thought you were a murderer."

"You had every right to wonder what had happened," he said, then paused. "Should we get in touch with your mom?"

Sara sighed. "Yeah. Will you wait with me, Dan?"

"Sure."

We stood there in silence while John went to call her mother. Sara looked lost.

"He hid his depression from me," she said softly. "It's why he understood me, I guess. I was just like him."

I glanced at her. "Just because you have the same disorder doesn't mean you're the same."

She kept her eyes on the tombstone. "I'm not a Star Child, Daniel."

She took off her bracelet, the little star charms dangling as she held it out and dropped it onto her father's grave. I didn't know what to say, so I just let the silence hang for a moment.

"I never really believed I was. I just read it once, and I liked it. It made me feel special."

"You are special," I said.

She shook her head, and her eyes were welling with tears again. "They had to protect me from the truth because they thought I couldn't handle it. I thought I was so smart. But I had it all wrong." She turned to me. "I'm alone. I always have been. I didn't talk to people because I thought being alone was safer. I was just Psycho Sara and I didn't talk and no one could tell me I wasn't special after all." Tears were streaming down her face now. "It was the only way."

"You were alone," I agreed. "But you're not anymore. I know your mom lied, but she was trying to protect you. And John . . . he seems like a decent guy."

She didn't say anything, so I reached out and squeezed her fingers.

"And I'm here too. You're weird and moody and maybe a little crazy, but you're also the most interesting person I've ever met. Trust me, you are special. And from now on, maybe you should stop trying so hard to be alone."

She smiled, and then squeezed my fingers back.

We walked out of the cemetery together, and she didn't cry anymore.

. . .

When her mom came home, I left. There was a big explosion of crying from her mom and grandma, and Sara just let them hug her, but I could see the anger in her eyes. I quietly slipped out, and John drove me home.

"Sorry I broke into your house," I said. "Three times."

He snorted. "That's fine. Bet you were pretty worried when I came in with the gun."

"Yeah."

He looked out at the dark sky. It was almost seven. "Relationships are tough, man."

"Seems that way."

"It's good that you're there for her. She needs someone. Take care of her."

I glanced at him. "We're not going out, you know."

He smiled. "Yeah. That's what they all say."

I frowned as we pulled into my driveway. I think my mom was watching from the window. She was probably freaked out and my phone had been off all day. Now there was a guy with tattoos dropping me off. I figured I'd better get in there before she hurried out.

"Thanks for the ride."

"Can I ask you something?"

I paused. "Sure."

"Do you think it was right? To cover it up? I mean, Michelle asked me. Did I do the right thing?"

I thought about that. "I don't know. It's tough to know what the right thing is."

He nodded and gestured to the house, where my mom was already opening the door. "No doubt. I hope it was. I was trying, you know. To be someone they could count on. I guess I messed it up."

I shrugged and slid out of the truck. "Either way, it's not too late to fix it."

I closed the door and hurried inside, and my mom gave John an inquisitive look and quickly closed the door behind me. After successfully avoiding most of her questions and escaping to my room, I decided to sit down at my laptop. It was time to finish the book.

CHAPTER 26

The apartment was quiet. The curtains were drawn tightly, and the room lay in heavy darkness. Behind them Daniel heard long fingernails tracing their way down the door. Checking, searching for an opening. Sara and Dan looked at each other, and then checked to make sure the door was locked.

"They'll find a way in soon," she said. "Let's go."

The living room was normal enough; quiet and empty. A half-drunk glass of water sat on the coffee table, collecting dust and slowly evaporating away.

"The bedroom," she said firmly.

Daniel followed her into the room. A small cot was tucked against the wall, and taking up the entire other half of the room was a massive set of screens and sensors and servers. It was the most impressive setup he had ever seen. Massive data lines ran into the walls, and on one of them was painted a symbol: a lone star. This was the center of the spiderweb. The station that connected to the rest. And according to Sara, it was the hidden gateway to another dimension.

One that Daniel could finally fix. He could bring them all back. He could save the world.

The switch was on the side of the computer—as clear as day. As Sara had said, it was down. Turned off.

When Charles Oliver had vanished, there had been no one here to reset it. Until now.

Sara turned to him and smiled. "You do the honors, Dan."

He nodded and started across the room. His footsteps creaked on the old floorboards.

As he approached the switch, he thought about the journey to get here. The creatures, the empty roads, the time he had spent with Sara. The feelings he had for her. The entire, difficult journey to fix his mistake. To find his destiny. To become the person he was meant to be.

The star grew bigger as he approached. It represented his extraordinary path.

It represented him and Sara. Star Kids. Heroes.

And all he had to do to fix it was flick the switch one more time.

I sat back for a second, my hands pausing on the keyboard. It was as if I had been writing and not even knowing what I saying. My hands were just moving. But now my brain had finally caught up to the story, and I felt like I was walking toward the star and the switch. And just then I realized how the story needed to end.

Daniel stopped. He looked at the switch, waiting for him.

"What's wrong?" Sara asked urgently.

The scratching at the door was getting louder. The creatures were closing in.

"I don't know."

She scowled. "Flick the switch! Everything will go back to normal. You can be a regular kid again."

He stood there for a moment longer. "No."

She hurried up beside him. "What?"

He shook his head. "I won't flick it. I like it here."

She looked confused. "We've come a long way for this. Have you looked outside lately? Humanity is gone. The world is empty. There are monsters attacking us right now. We're going to die."

He turned to her and smiled. "It's us against the world. We're not alone anymore."

Sara frowned. "What would we do?"

"Anything," Daniel replied. "We don't need anyone else. We can take on the monsters."

He reached out and took Sara's hand.

"What do you think? Us against the world."

"Dan?"

I turned to the bedroom door. It was Emma.

"Yeah?"

"Do you want to read for a bit?" She was holding her book under her arm.

I looked at her for a moment. I guess my ending wasn't the right solution. Sure, it was kind of cool to think of facing an empty world with Sara. But I didn't really want that. I didn't want to be alone. I would miss Emma and my parents and even Steve. I would miss Max and Tuesday video games and everything else.

I smiled. "Sure."

I turned back to the computer as she went and lay down on the carpet.

Sara squeezed Daniel's hand and smiled, the croquet mallet still slung over her shoulder. "It can still be me and you," she said. "We'll take on the world. But first we have to bring it back."

Daniel thought about that, and then nodded. "Together?"

"Together," she agreed.

They walked to the switch on the computer, put their fingers on the switch, and turned it on. Instantly a pale, bone-thin man appeared in the chair. He looked at them and nodded.

"How long were we gone?" he asked quietly.

"A few days," Sara said.

"Felt like I blinked," he murmured. "Fascinating. Do me a favor . . . don't flick that switch again."

Daniel smiled grimly. "I won't."

They walked down the hallway, watching as people started leaving their apartments, looking completely normal. They walked outside into the brilliant daylight, and the streets were already bustling. The moon was gone.

Daniel looked around the chaotic city streets.

He took Sara's hand again, and for the first time in years—since long before he'd ever flicked the switch—he didn't feel alone.

I smiled and saved it. Not great. Not really. It didn't have the right character development, and the story needed work, and I wasn't sure I liked the title. But I liked the ending. For me it meant everything.

I lay down on the carpet next to Emma.

"I see a fairy," she said. "Elleor. A fern-child from Laron who fell for a human prince."

I smiled. "I see a prince. Logan. He has dark hair and blue eyes. He just saw himself for the first time."

We opened our books and started to read. I fell asleep with the book on my chest, and when I woke up, I was lying in bed. My dad must have put me there. I got up and started the Routine.

CHAPTER 27

Monday was a strange day at school. I guess I was popular now. Taj and Tom were talking to me and parading around the school with their medals, and they invited me to play basketball and never said a word when I missed a layup. Max was as happy as I'd ever seen him.

After the state championship game the high school coach had come over and said how excited he was to see Max the next year. There had even been a few college scouts in the stands, and a couple of them had introduced themselves as well. Max had a bright future. And his dad had watched it all, and I know for Max that was the most important thing.

Raya came over at first recess. Her hair was curled a little today, sweeping in toward her chin.

"You must have had some weekend," she said.

I smirked. "You could say that."

"Must be weird . . . being the team hero."

"It was one kick," I said. "Max won the game for us."

She smiled and gave me a little push. "It was a nice kick."

I knew those little pushes. It was classic flirting. I'd read it in an online fashion magazine.

"Thanks," I said. "I try."

"I told my dad you won the game," she said, smiling. "He said he still doesn't like you."

I laughed. "Fair enough."

"But that makes you the rebel, you know."

"What can I say? Fathers everywhere are terrified of me."

As we laughed, I saw Sara at the far end of the yard. She was sitting on a bench, her TA next to her. She looked like I remembered. Eyes distant. Alone. She was everything I was afraid of being.

"Can you excuse me for a second?" I said.

Raya looked at me in surprise. "Of course."

I walked across the yard alone. The basketball game continued on loudly behind me.

I didn't look back.

She didn't even notice me until I was right in front of her. And then her eyes widened. A smile tugged at her lips. Her TA looked at me and then at her phone.

"Just going to take a call," she said, and hurried away.

"Hey," I said.

"Hey."

"How are you?"

She shrugged. "Okay. Still weird with my mom. But maybe it will get better eventually."

I nodded and sat down next to her. "Yeah."

"Shouldn't you be hanging out with your friends?"

"I am."

She giggled, sounding like a thirteen-year-old girl for once. Then she looked at me.

"They're going to make fun of you. You're hanging with Psycho Sara."

I shrugged. "Oh, well. If you're a psycho, then so am I. Deranged Daniel. What do you think?"

"I hate it."

I laughed. "Me too. Listen . . . I thought maybe I would talk to my parents about going with you at some point. To that group."

"Really?" she asked, surprised. "Why?"

"Because even though we're extraordinary, I think we could still use a little help."

We sat there for a while and watched the younger grades run around.

"So would it be like . . . a date?" Sara asked.

"We would be going to see a therapist."

"It could still count."

I smiled and shook my head. "Yeah. I guess it could be a date. Oh, and before I forget." I took her bracelet out of my pocket and handed it to her. I had picked it up when Sara wasn't looking.

She took it hesitantly, looking at me. "I'm not a Star Child, remember?"

I grinned and took another bracelet out of my pocket. Actually it was just a piece of string with a paper clip folded into a star as a charm, but it was the best I could do on short notice. I slipped it on.

"Of course we are," I replied. "Tenant number one. You are a Star Child for life."

Sara grinned, and her eyes fogged up just a little. Without warning she hugged me tightly. I knew people were probably watching, but for once I didn't care.

Two nights later my mom, Emma, Steve, and I had dinner. My dad was at work and would be home late as usual. Steve was wolfing down some spaghetti so that he could go out, and my mom was talking to Emma about a project at school. I just sat there and ate, thinking.

I spent so much time hiding my OCD from them. I thought I was different or special or crazy and I didn't want anyone else to know. I was just like Sara. But it was exhausting.

"So what did you and Sara do tonight?" my mom asked.

I hadn't told her about the therapy session. Baby steps.

"Just hung out," I said.

"I can't believe Daniel has a girlfriend," Steve said.

I scowled. "We're friends."

"Sure," he replied. Emma giggled.

"Do you think she might . . . start talking more to us?" my mom asked carefully.

"I think so," I said. "She's working on it."

The front door suddenly opened, and I heard my dad step in. My mom looked up in surprise.

"You're home early," she said as my dad strolled into the kitchen.

"Caught an earlier train," he replied. He mussed up my hair, which was sort of weird and nice. "There's the champ. The team still celebrating, or you back to practicing?"

"Still celebrating," I said, and he smiled and went to grab a plate. I realized right then that maybe it wasn't the football he cared about. Maybe that was just the way he connected to me, since we didn't have much else in common. As he sat down at the head of the table, I thought back to my book. I had long ago convinced myself that my dad only liked football, and Steve hated me, and my mom just cared about Emma. I had been making myself disappear.

"So what are we talking about?" my dad said.

I smiled. I wasn't ready to tell them about the OCD yet—I still needed time and it was all too new. But suddenly I knew I could tell them at any time, and that they would still be there. I wouldn't be alone anymore.

"We were talking about Daniel's girlfriend," Steve said. "I think they're getting serious."

"Really?" my dad asked, turning to me with interest. "Did you go on a date or something?"

I gave Steve a resigned look. "Can we change the subject?"

Before bed I started editing my book. I read somewhere that editing should take at least twice as long as writing the book, so I figured I had better get started. There were a lot of mistakes. Actually it didn't sound great now that I read it again, but that was all right. I would just keep editing it until it did, I guess.

I decided to keep the book title for now—*The Last Kid on Earth.* It kind of fit. He was always the last kid on earth in his own mind, even before he flicked the switch. He lived in his own world, and it was empty. But then he invited Sara with the explosive croquet mallet into it, and he didn't feel so alone. I liked that part.

I closed the laptop and stood up, stretching. I knew what was next, of course. I would go to the bathroom and start the Routine. I had to do it. If I didn't, I would die.

I thought back to group. To waiting for my mom to pick us up.

Sara had made me promise to text her before I started. That was it. Just text her.

I fidgeted for a moment, and then grabbed my cell.

I'm about to start.

I waited for a moment. There was no reply. She must have been asleep. I sighed and put the phone down. Changing into my sleep pants, I got ready for the Routine. I felt my eyes welling with tears.

For just a moment I thought maybe I could beat it.

I was starting for the door when my phone buzzed. I stopped and picked it up.

Turn your light off and lie down.

I frowned. *I can't.*

Just for a bit. You can do your routine after. Please.

I hesitated, and then turned the light off and climbed into bed. I felt my skin prickling and my stomach hurt, but it was only for a bit. I could fix it after.

Okay. I'm in bed.

Good. If you get up . . . text me.

Okay.

I pulled the covers up. I was shaking now.

You're going to be all right.

I hope so.

Good night, OCDaniel.

I laughed. She hated "Deranged Daniel" so much that she had made me a new name.

Good night, Psycho Sara.

I put the phone beside me and decided I was going to wait as long as I could. I had to try.

I read the text again and smiled. Something else occurred to me.

We were only crazy when we thought we were alone. Now there were two of us, and we were both perfectly normal in each other's eyes. And to me, there in the dark, that meant everything.

Author's Note

The Daniel in this story is in many ways an almost autobiographical representation of myself at that age. I too spent as many as five hours every night trying to get to bed. I too suffered from panic attacks, anxiety, and derealization. Several times a day I felt as if I were dying — something I later learned was caused by anxiety and panic attacks—and I began to use ritualized compulsions to try and deal with the terror. Until I was almost sixteen, I had no idea what I was dealing with. I thought I was damaged and cursed. I kept it a secret from everyone, even my parents. I felt alone.

Obsessive Compulsive Disorder (OCD) is one of the most common and least understood mental illnesses in the world today. "I am so OCD" has become a popular saying to describe someone who likes things ordered and clean. But OCD is not liking things clean or organizing your socks. It is a constant battle with your mind that can afflict every minute of every day. Daniel, for example, struggled to ignore desperate urges to flick lights, count, and repeat actions. And for most people—especially adolescents—it is a battle fought in absolute secrecy.

That is a common story of OCD sufferers. We don't want to be called crazy. We don't want to be ostracized. I guarded my secret until my late twenties, when I finally sought help. The struggle to deal with anxiety disorders and depression isn't and *shouldn't* be a solitary one. This is a story about hope and acceptance. It is my wish that anyone struggling with mental illness who reads this realizes that there are many other people out there in the same situation, and just as importantly, that there are people that want to help. My OCD is a challenge that I deal with every day, but I wrote this book because I believe it can be defeated. If you are dealing with a mental illness, don't be ashamed to ask for help. Remember: you are not alone.

If you have questions or want to seek help for yourself or someone you know, talk to your doctor (who can refer you to a trained psychologist) or visit the International OCD Foundation online at iocdf.org for information and support groups in your area.